M000296081

This poet's take on the demanding gan
sensations and images, history and wor
moments that leave you gasping or scr
ball with a bat, you know *the freedom of m.* ...... g..... ....
William's paean to the gritty players and everyday heroes in a league
where baseball's not a commodity but a dream come true or about to in
the next play proves over and over that *joy never loses.*
--Gwynn O'Gara

Timothy William's *Baseball: In and Out of Time* is pure diamond magic. I
was entranced from the first pitch and could smell the cut grass, feel the
tightness of anticipation and silent fear, sting of the errors, and scattered
cheers across the years. This old ball player simply loved it.
-- Alex Call

Timothy Williams' new book of prose and poems titled, *Baseball: In and
Out of Time*, is a muscular, musical collection about baseball and life that
bridges the chasms dividing game and reality, time and leisure,
philosophy and frolic. There, poems sing in voices that straddle multiple
certainties. Lyrically compiled, the images speak of fire, smoke, heat,
politics, love, and history in such a way that we are unaware we are being
illuminated on the mysteries of life.
-- Ken Rodgers

To those of us who have known him well, it's been no secret that
Timothy Williams loves baseball. Now, he's put his passion for the All-
American game into a beautiful book in which he introduces readers to
some of the colorful ballplayers he has known both on and off the field.
They're a wonderfully drawn case of characters and, whether you're a
baseball fan or not, this book is bound to delight. Baseball has been
written about so often that it's a challenge to write about it newly and
freshly. Timothy Williams has done that here. He presents baseball in a
new light through the eyes of an artist and a philosopher. This book is a
bases-loaded home run.
-- Jonah Raskin

La poesía de Timothy Williams me recordó a mi papá, quien juega al béisbol también en una liga de adultos mayores de edad. Nunca había leído acerca de esto: qué lindo que Williams haya escrito sobre este tema para que más gente mayor de edad—ambos mujeres y hombres— puedan involucrarse con este deporte tan bonito.

(Timoty Williams' poetry reminds me of my father, who also plays baseball in a senior league. I have never read anything about this: how lovely that Williams has written about this topic so that seniors—both men and women—can get invovled in this wonderful sport.)
--Gabriela Bayona

Baseball

In and Out of Time:

A Rookie's Journey in the Senior Leagues

Timothy Williams

JAXON'S
PRESS

Cover Art: Vita Sehagen, Amsterdam, 2017

Cover Design: Timothy Williams

Editor-in-Chief Alison Jacobs Maldonado

Spanish Translations by Alison Jacobs Maldonado

Photo of Larry Hendrickson courtesy Larry and MSBL Photography

Publisher: Timothy Williams
Jaxon's Press, Santa Rosa, California
jaxonspress@gmail.com/707 321-3852

SECOND EDITION

First Printing

Library of Congress Control Number: 9781737834939

ISBN 978-1-7378349-3-9

Acknowledgements

Many thanks to: The Redwood Empire Baseball League, rebl.org, and the players, friends, and coaches I've played with along the way, including: Don and Shari DeCordova, Dick Giberti, Dan (Dano) Lepez, David Smith, Lou Patler, Larry Hendrickson, David (Doc) Charp, Allan Green, left handed curveball artist, Jesse Bower, Rick Harmon, George Curtis, Joseph Svetlik, and Art Hernandez, a Legacy Division player who has played for more than 30 years straight—who also retrieved my home run ball from a parking lot at ASU—Mike McKeever, John Sensenbaugh, Geno Soldate, Wes Logan, Ron Starkey, Greg Peterson, Bill Furbush, Sam Cardenas, Randy Blossom, Tom Ribbecke, Lowell Stalbaum, Big Al Surges, Willard Ferrell, Ladd Miyasaki, Jim Maresca, Rick Mercurio, Rick Chassey, Jim Sullens, Commissioner Rick Cantor, players named in the text, and too many to say including the good fellow, Wayne Pellow. And to all the past and future REBL players, this book's for you.

Extra Gratitude for: Ralph Leef, Sarah Estalee Baker, Jonah Raskin, Alex Call, Gwynn O'Gara, Ken Rodgers, Nathan (N8) Elder, Gabriela Bayona.

Joe Lind's character is based on a real person, Joe Lindquist.

Otto is a fictional character. Any resemblance to a real, living person is purely coincidental.

Foreword

It feels strange to be asked to write the foreword for a book written by a gentleman I have only conversed with while standing on first base during Redwood Empire Baseball League (REBL) games over the past few years: Timothy Williams, the first baseman for the 65-and-over Blues, and myself, a slap-hitting leadoff hitter for the Jazz, who holds the record for the REBL single-season batting average of .703. I have spent nearly 40 years as a sportswriter for *The Press Democrat*, covering the San Francisco Giants when Willie Mays, McCovey, Cepeda and company were the talk of Northern California—and then the Oakland A's when "Catfish" Hunter, Sal Bando, and diminutive Campy Campaneris were at their best. At this point in my career, I feel honored to introduce this journey into "old man baseball" played on crab-grass-filled city and high school diamonds in Sonoma and Marin Counties. Yet, there are exceptions: Recreation Park in Healdsburg, A Place to Play in Santa Rosa, and Sonoma State University, to name a few.

I actually knew more about Timothy then he realized as we chatted for a few moments at first because a teammate of mine had pointed out the lanky first baseman and said he was quite the poet. An enthusiast at graphic art and an in-depth reader, I was intrigued. It was after we became "friends" on Facebook that I quickly realized how talented my baseball bud was, especially when I read his book, *Figure on The Road*, centering on the California wildfires that devastated his own beloved Lake County and prompted melancholic feelings for a lost era of his youth. I couldn't put the book down, finishing—quite satisfied—in less than two hours.

In this new book, Timothy utilizes his poetry and prose to chronicle his introduction into the senior baseball league with more than 700 participants, ages 18-86. Yes, 86! The main characters—ageless Dick Giberti, Dano Lepez, David Smith, and Lou Patler of the 2008 Oaks— made me laugh as I read of their exploits as seen from the eyes of a 65-something "rookie" teammate and author. In these days of instant gratification, $300 million contracts, and fast-talking sports analysts, media outlets snub their nose at senior athletics, although there are some great stories to be told. But the REBL isn't about public notoriety or filling the stands for the games played almost every Sunday from early April to early October. It is about staying young at heart.

Timothy Williams, who has greeted hundreds of opponents at his bag on the right side of the infield—some smiling in wonderment that they singled to left when they were trying to go to the opposite side and some so serious that they only grunted in response—has gotten down and dirty. He's painted a picture with his prose that brings the game alive for anyone who has ever played. I came away feeling like I had to wipe crud away from a dirty uniform following a poorly executed slide into second base.

Having recently moved to a state that doesn't have nearly the size and organization of the REBL, I told my wife as my 75th birthday drew close that I was probably done playing baseball. After reading this book, I have decided to put off such a drastic decision until I turn 80— the spirit in the great beyond (and a cranky left knee) willing.

Ralph Leef
Denver, Colorado
September 13, 2023

Baseball
In and Out of Time:

A Rookie's Journey in the Senior Leagues

"It ain't over till it's over."

—Yogi Berra

"Baseball is a humbling game."

Timothy J. Hannan

Contents

Introduction

National senior baseball leagues are open doors to any person's dreams of playing real baseball. If you know someone wanting to jump into games, growing tired of watching from the sidelines, and thinking they're over the hill or too tired, encourage them to think again: why not try out for a roster spot in a senior baseball league?

The Redwood Empire Baseball League (REBL) began as a collective dream in Sonoma County, California, in 1989. Mike Zaccagna called a few friends to meet at McNear's Saloon and Dining House, a stone's throw from the Petaluma River and the train tracks that run beside it, in Historic Downtown Petaluma, California.[i] In Petaluma's active oceanic air, the breezy eatery was the ideal place to sketch a dream that has lasted more than 30 years and counting. On the pub's paper napkins, the group wrote names of people who might want to play baseball in the new REBL.[ii] Two semi-pro league players, Brad Silva and Larry Hendrickson, began as rookies for the REBL in 1990. The pioneer baseball league was organized with umpires and teams with uniforms. The games were played on Rancho Cotate High School's J.V. and Varsity fields. As unique situations called for participation, some days the players became the grounds crews themselves. Ernie Nackord and Zeke Zaccagna chalked the baselines some nights, aided by the headlights of their trucks, to get the fields ready for the morning games. The REBL was born.[iii]

The league became a place to play after high school, college, semi-pro leagues, and the big leagues, as well as for players who lived outside any league, like me. I had never played baseball after ninth grade, except

i

in games and workouts that I organized from San Francisco to Lake County, California with friends on a vacant field in Petaluma, a meadow on Bottle Rock Road on Cobb Mountain, the Memorial Amphitheater atop Mount Tamalpais, Mission Dolores Park in San Francisco, Albert's Field and Dominican College in San Rafael, Doyle Park in Santa Rosa, and Middletown High School. For decades, you'd find me pitching batting practice to a few of my friends anywhere flat or—if we found a school field with a mound—after hours on empty, warm summer evenings.

In 1992, my desire to play baseball led to the REBL home fields of Rancho Cotate High School for a tryout, on the edge of Sonoma State University. It was flat land with red dirt, baselines, backstop, and grandstands for friends and families to sit. A group of 20 guys showed up for the tryouts. At that time, I was 43. There was one division, 30+. We fielded ground balls, pitched off the mound, ran bases, and chased fly balls. That day is brighter than the sun in most memories. It carried me from makeshift sandlot games with a few friends and into the real world of playing baseball.

Women are welcome to play as well, and some have. Three decades ago, I played in an after-the-season-ended, makeshift game at Redwood High School in Marin County with a woman in her 30s. She made throws and covered shortstop as well as or better than any 30 to 40-something player. When I first noticed her, and no doubt she spent idle moments watching players observing her, I knew it was a proud moment for senior league baseball to build on.

My experiences of entering, exiting, and returning to senior baseball[iv] inspired me to write a Players' Edition in 2010, and grow that into this Second Edition in 2023. The batting practices, games, and fellow players who have become life-long friends were recalled from notes, memories, and conversations.

When it came time to publish this book, set in the Great Recession of 2008 as the housing bubble collapsed and homeowners abandoned their mortgages, I chose to create a want-to-be player named Jim Linehan to embody my experiences as a rookie. I was 59 and playing in a 45+ league. This book follows my ventures through injuries, health setbacks, self-doubt, determination to succeed, inspiring friendships, a life-long brother-pal named Joe, and a single foe, Otto—a fictional character with antagonistic undertones.

Just show up, try out, and give it your best despite the odds. You may be out of time when you get here, but you'll be in time when you leave.

Warm Up

The conversation of ball and glove begins on the outfield grass. Gloves pop; leather claps serially down the line. Time's other clock, the one that beats a polyphonic rhythm, begins here on the outfield grass. Over the fence, the world travels faster than arms can throw, while under the sky, teammates watch ground and air for the slightest movement of a baseball. Like a mockingbird's morning song or the crows' warrior chant at sundown, sounds erupting from a baseball park are an ageless murmur of the natural world.

The new season starts slowly for Cookie, Slick, and Dano's team—the Oaks, a team of loyal guys in their 60s who play hardball in the Redwood Empire Baseball League (REBL). The layoff period has added a layer of fat to each player, and it takes weeks of practice to shed the long winter of food and drink. No sweat, for an easy sun follows the team's path as they warm up. Players throw, field, and run to get into "baseball shape."

Oaks' players endeavor to fuse individual and common purpose with the grit, skill, and art of the game at hand. The outside world of families, jobs, and bills awaits their return. They have learned baseball's time-altering nature. Hours become months, decades, and lifetimes. No matter what age, sex, or level of play, the tools are the same: bat, ball, glove, and tight-fitting shoes.

Through bright daylight, the baseball is barely visible, like a sunspot appearing in a flaming mass. When a fly ball crosses into the sun, it takes a camera's eye to catch it. Or drop it.

Kicking dirt around first base, a rookie, listening to a tune in his head, takes throws from the infielders. A tall lefty, you can tell he's as stiff-jointed and skinny as a foul pole. What brought him back to baseball at this stage of his life, no one knows. He takes a throw, watching the ball spin into the pocket.

The second baseman, Dave "Wolverine" Woltering, throws a gas pedal, the further along it travels, the faster it accelerates in the soft air. The ball glances off the lefty's mitt and dents him on the bridge of his nose. The rookie grabs his glasses, slamming them on the ground. Dent draws blood. Dano barks, "You'd better go to the hospital. Do you want a driver?" "No," Jim replies, and reluctantly bounds away in his midnight blue Volvo sedan.

For some guys, senior baseball began after shaking Dano's hand, including Jim during his first rookie year in '92. Despite citing his and Jim's early years as some of his favorite times, Dano intends to drive baseball ghosts out of past glories and onto today's ball field.

*****

Perennial starter and All Star, Timothy J. Hannan, steps onto this year's infield. The rookie eventually calls Hannan "Redwood Hannan," because he looms large with a bat in his hands and sports curly, cropped hair, the color of redwoods—a few shades darker than New York Mets legendary first baseman/outfielder, Rusty Staub. Like Rusty Staub and Tim Hannan have done many times, Tim smashed a two-bagger over third base last year. However, digging out of the box, his Achilles parted from the bone and he collapsed three feet from home plate. He sat out the year anchored in a plaster-of-Paris boot. Of that experience and other snapshots during the course of 20 seasons, Hannan routinely says, "Baseball is a humbling game."

The Oaks' line-up boasts the oldest players in the REBL. Caps off and one sees balding, grey heads and cool telepathic eyes. The ruddy smile lines baked into their faces reveal decades in the sun. Yet another edge of the diamond must be chiseled to play the game as long as one possibly can. One October, the Oaks manager, Dick Giberti, called "Slick" by most players, cut a new diamond. He celebrated his 70th year by pitching a no-hitter in the senior World Series in Arizona. A decade later, we celebrated his 80th year as he pitched against a team called the Blues on a field at Santa Rosa High School. Chris Smith, of Santa Rosa's *Press Democrat*, covered the milestone.

*****

After the rookie takes flight to the ER, Hannan's first baseman's mitt breaks the silence. Meanwhile, at the clinic, the rookie's eyes purple up, but once he starts driving back to G. Park, he forgets the dent. He finds a bench in an inconsolable world of pain and watches players take ground balls, stretching last year's arms to new lengths. Rookie Jim watches through rheumy eyes that burn and betray him. What these guys want to do is play baseball until November. And until they die. "I don't know if I'm up for this," he says, gauze taped across his nose and cheeks, to no one listening or sitting beside him in the dugout.

The dugout is a long, confining, and oddly comforting hotel room of sorts with a view of the first base side of the infield through chain-link fencing. Jim is spellbound by the errant order of baseball sundries: hanging equipment bags with airport wheels, bats leaning on the bottom

3

half of the screen, a few custom-made bats with players' names, and boutique insignias from all over the country. Jim picks up a scuffed ball from the bucket of Rawlings. A mixture of old and new, a few are still wrapped in cellophane, inked with the REBL logo, a stadium blueprint with two bats like a scripted X in a prehistoric font. The MSBL logo jumps out, and the signature of the Steve Sigler, the National founder, makes it official. Jim keeps the old ball in his hand and later carries it to his truck.

He surveys the disordered canvas duffel bags and spies the snack foods reeking of urban-in-a-rural-setting-ballpark smells sandwiched in between open packs and coolers. Hard boiled eggs with their pithy whiffs and their sidekick, a Leslie saltshaker, salmon toast in unwrapped parchment paper, celery sticks and melting peanut butter, cylinders of crackers, wedges of brie, amassed quarts of neon green, blue, and orange Gatorade, and one opened tin of chili. Jim isn't even aware that he's still sitting with that old baseball and looking through the screens, like veils of resistance that keep him from playing.

As time on the field passes slowly through the hands of his teammates, he can't help wondering, "why do folks in their 60s risk injury to play baseball in a 45-and-over league?" Because rare and ancient wolves howl in their dreams in the middle of the night? Call it hunger—a hunger that salivates the more the player makes a good catch, gets a key hit, or performs one of the endless nuances it takes to refine the game. Like Slick backing up the plate on a throw home or Dano bunting a runner over when every fielder in the ballpark had back-paddled, figuring he'd swing away.

Jim snaps out of his daydreaming and turns his head towards the action of a practice game. The runner on first base takes his lead. All eyes bear down on the batter. Crack. A sharp ground ball to the third baseman, Tim McGaw, who charges and snags the ball below his knees. He pivots on the run and slings the ball to the second baseman; Tim nails the runner by six feet.

McGaw's demeanor is that of a gentleman more than a pigpen, but he tramps around in a filthy uniform after the fifth inning. Radar in his brain, he runs through the ball like a timed train. On the next pitch, he cradles the grounder as if it were a new-born daughter and lets the ball fly in a straight arrow. Not much arc in his heave across this diamond to first base. Two outs. Add quickness to spring feet and you have an infielder. Throw wool-soft hands into the mix, and you have an All Star. Observe the hitter in a clean uniform running down the line and freezing suddenly, like an ice sculpture. His face hollows, his teeth grind, his hat lowers in resignation. Read his lips as he tells himself, "Don't hit it to McGaw."

*****

Soul searching in the dugout, "I still don't know if I'm up for this," Jim says to no one all over again. Looking back a few weeks to the day a teammate wound up in the hospital after a game at El Molino High School, he remembers Lou Patler. He had it worse than these two black eyes. After the game, Lou and a teammate had driven home to Marin County. In the car, it hit him; Lou's hands felt stabbing needles, and his feet tingled and numbed. In the ER, they hooked him up to an EKG and checked out his heart. Everything turned out okay, but the news dropped a lead weight of dread into Jim and the rest of the team's collective gut.

5

These ballplayers show up to play with wide and varied health ailments. What's reassuring to Jim is there are at least two physicians in this league, and one is his teammate, David Smith. The other, a player on the Dirt Dogs, is David Charp, a splendid pitcher with heavy eyebrows and country doctor demeanor, affectionately called, well, Doc. He reminds all players—regardless of ability or team affiliations—to eat broccoli because he's never unearthed a trace of broccoli in a cadaver.

And Dano has always said, "Baseball teaches you what's wrong with you." You can name the health conditions from A to Z. And players learn to play with the knowledge of their own limitations. On the other hand, some players feel, "if one can't live one's dream no matter what the age, why live at all?" Still others call it quits after a surgery or an illness. It's often too much for their families to overcome.

As Jim recalls Patler's injury, Lou is driving north from Mill Valley, California, on Highway 101 to the Oaks' practice as if his truck knew the way and he was blindfolded. His pickup slows and ambles into the lot at G. Park. He thumps the door shut and threads through the parked cars to the infield. Before crossing the first base line, he stops and breathes and blows, his head at a slight upward gaze, his hand flat across his eyebrows, straining to see where his inner baseball field joins his outer elation. The blue spring air brightens above the sweat and grime of players getting into baseball shape and swagger in left field. Their broad forms rise and fall with each throw. Deep green turf and the warm sun cast a generous universe. The smell of cut grass creates its own path to the heart. It lives somewhere, a few steps up from the persuasions of isolation, growing old, and shuffling around with the modern computer droop—slumped shoulders and a spine shaped like the letter C.

Jim's still watching the field through two black eyes, figuring it all out. Is it worth the work? It's like having a second or third job. Is it worth the hospital visits? Both his wife and grown son have always given him the mythological chartreuse light. His friends, too. "Play ball," they say.

He sits. He watches. These outfielders push their chests out when emanating oxygen-charged release. They're driven competitors and respire air to lighten their numerous burdens. Their instincts are aligned to stretch, leap, or drop like a hawk on a loose ball. They seem to make a certain play, whatever that play may be, better than the last time they made it. Or for that matter, better than anyone else in the park that day.

As Lou steps onto the field, for the first time since his ER visit, someone yells, "Time out!" The team rallies across the infield and encircles Lou as if the game ended and he got the winning hit. Shouting, arms ahigh, patting him on the back, "Hey Lou, I see you're over the hospital food. No more IVs, eh?" "You're looking better than the rumors," says another. "That's because I'm here, fellas. Good to be back."

A voice rises in the mix, "Do you want to do anything, throw some BP (batting practice), maybe swing the bat?" Someone flips him a ball which his hand reaches for like a handshake. He does seem a little lost without uniform and hat, but that changes quickly once he begins to rub up the ball.

"No, I can't right now. I want to play catch." Lou is known around the league as a "work horse." When he played third or shortstop, he threw a heavy ball; it smacked the glove, sounding like a 10-pound

7

weight hitting a garage door. Now, throwing soft toss with eyes open wide, a rounded figure in the full light, he's living the dream of playing catch again. As if a smithy in a past life, his decades in the sun pound away at the comeback question. It's the same question that's in Jim's soul search engine.

Four years earlier, when the rookie came back to play for Dragons South and he wound up in the hospital, Lou pitched 43 innings. He was second only to team leader, Slick Giberti, who threw 84 innings and had a remarkable 2.25 ERA in what's called a hitter's league. In a lineup of trusty bats, Lou held down a .361 average. Jim's question hauls his heart aboard the comeback train to accompany his sense of reason.

Can I really play baseball with high caliber players like these? Am I so afraid of failure or even, success, that I won't even take a gamble? Would I rather dream and remember the old days?

On this warm spring day, Lou returns to the shaded dugout after 10 minutes of soft toss and visiting the wanderings of his last 50 years, including the knee injury that kept him from playing professionally with the Detroit Tigers. He paces as if determined to dissolve all doubt of his return to the field again. But he already knows the answer.

He sits next to the rookie, whose turmoil is showing signs of releasing its hold. Once the heart comes into play, reason doesn't stand a chance. Lou, arm on the rookie's shoulder, grins, and in a singing voice, says, "We've got to be crazy to play this game." Jim sensed that Lou wanted to add, "at our age," but censored himself. Now they are both beaming at the prospect of being at the ballpark. Watching the players picking up grounders and making throws, their patience—waiting for the love of the game to return—offers errant moments of transcendence.

Lou rises and leaves the meditations of the bench and follows the path back to the parking lot. Looking over his shoulder, he cheers his team as they line up to take infield. A lot of baseball to play yet. As far as the rookie with two black eyes? Let's see what he can do.

Hola Lou

Gracias por tener el corazón que no se hundió.
Estás recogiendo pelotas del suelo en campocorto profundo.
Disparas una bala de cañón que envía el bolsillo al hueso.
El corredor está fuera y todavía estás de pie.

*****

Lou está en el plato, batallando por su vida.
La próxima temporada, estará de nuevo en la caja de bateo,
tan rápido como el gruñido de un gato montés.

Hey Lou

Thanks for having the heart that didn't go down.
You're scooping grounders at deep short.
You fire a cannonball to first that drives the pocket to the bone.
The runner's out and you're still standing.

*****

Lou's at home plate, battling for his life.
Next season, he'll be back in the batter's box,
quick as a mountain cat's growl.

Baseball in Today's Time

Out of the blue sky, Joseph Lind, a neighborhood guy and old friend of Jim's he hasn't seen in 20 years—wearing a broad and blue Hawaiian shirt—walks right into the dugout, halts, and with hands on hips, glares at Jim as if to say, "don't you know me?" Soaked in half sun and half shade, he's six feet two and is a wide, big-boned guy with thick forearms, rocky-blue eyes, and dirty blond hair. Nicknamed, The Swede, his jaw juts like a power hitter and he smells faintly of the amber glow of whiskey.

"Hey, Swede!" Jim's seen those thick forearms before, at Albert's Park in San Rafael in the '70s, holding a bat. Jim had thrown a pitch, and after Joe hit it over two fences, it clanged onto the metal roof of the tool shed by the tennis courts. Now, Jim stands up—and the two ballplayers, hands over shoulders—are back patting in the dugout.

Joseph Lind says he's followed the REBL since 1995, the year after Jim walked away from the game. "What's up with your nose?" Joe asks.

"I didn't see a ball coming," Jim answers.

"I saw it hit you. You took one for the team, but the team got nothing out of it. That's why I showed up to see how you're doing. Your eyes are black and purple—you look like a raccoon."

"So I hear," Jim says.

"You could use a medicinal." Joe pulls out a pewter hip flask, with enough patina to qualify as an essential ingredient for more than one century, from his back pocket and dangles it in front of Jim's nose. "Nice fragrance, eh? Have a taste of the best Irish whiskey around."

Jim waves him off. "No booze in the dugout. This isn't a brew league."

"True," Joe asserts, "You won't find coolers of beer in the dugout or the stands; but I've seen a few guys sneak a sole shot. You may get a whiff of one now and then."

"I already have, Joe. When you showed up."

Joe holds the contoured hip flask up at eye level. Sunlight smudges pale shapes into its timeworn sheen and—like an adman—declares, "Tullamore D.E.W., a caramelly cure."

"Where the hell have you been, Joe?"

"I don't play anymore, but that's a different story." Joe quickly slugs the flask and shoves it into his pocket. He starts talking where Lou left off, as if he had overheard their trepidations and resolutions in the dugout. He raises his arms towards the sun. Standing and stretching to the sky, he nods and paces the dugout, looking out on the field and back at Jim. "I figured you needed a talking to; this isn't the '90s—you don't know anybody here."

"I know Dano."

"Ever hear of Allan Green, the Dragons' player/manager?"

"Nope."

"He plays a great game and builds winning teams. He is kind of reserved and studious, but he leads by example. His teams model respect for the player and the game itself. He's the best scout in the league for tracking down high-level talent. Even former professionals."

Joe sits next to Jim and examines his eyes: lava layers of purple and puffed sacks of swollen skin surround half closed lids. "You better get some ice on that."

Jim answers in a gravelly voice, "Ah, yes, I'm back in the REBL, the world of fire and ice."

"Take a second look at the REBL, my friend," Joe replies, "and a long look at Larry Hendrickson working the mound right now; hear how he growls at the release on his follow through?" They look out at the field and fall silent.

"See his edge?" Joe continues. "It's as necessary as a controlled burn in fire season. A competitor with a routine. Composed, like a surgeon. His incisions are strikeouts."

"I know him from '92 when he pitched for the Phillies. I remember striking out, too. A fastball in my eyes. Two swift strikes and a changeup. My bat stopped dead halfway through strike three. The wrists hurt for two days."

"He speeds it up and takes his foot off the gas. He's not gangly or wild. His power is poise, form, and polish."

Their eyes find the field again. Nothing but todays and tomorrows in slow motion. The story doesn't end in '92.

Joe rises, paces the dugout. Eyes straight ahead. Finches dart into the rosemary bushes. He stops and watches.

Joe resumes his flask as if he's taking a sacred moment for the finches and melancholy effects of aging and turns his body back toward the mesh. On the field, a batter is spraying hits. Jim pipes up, "batting practice is for the hitter to find his swing, not the pitcher to show off his curveball."

Joe turns and paces like a caged lion back the other way, scratching his arms and his ears, staring up, and blinking his eyes through thoughts. "Baseball has lines as borders, but the ball itself doesn't always

15

travel in a straight line." He looks back at Jim, who sits upright, arms held away from his sides, squeezing the bench with both hands so his knuckles turn pale yellow and white.

"Some at-bats you never forget," Jim remarks.

"Albert's Park—off you—was my best." Joe says.

Jim hears a form of music as if it were played in an outdoor theater. On the edge of the bench, he tilts back his head, left ear stuck on the infield radio of sounds. Because to him, baseball is art and is especially musical. As a child, he listened when his neighbors sang "Fly Me to The Moon" on summer nights in Cobb Mountain, California.

Here G. Park, he hears the melodies of bats. They repeat scuffled or steady knocks on the door or flat duds, whose long-low frequencies and energy-sapping collision thunks vibrate^v convincingly enough to sting your hands. He hears loud contact of the seasoned veterans' bats and the crash of wooden mallets—striking pallets of folded chairs. When the bat meets the core and the ball strikes the nodes—or the screws—called—the sweet spot—the real music begins. On the bat's pop, he hears that sharp crack and the dimmed fade of the ball sailing away. Eventually rundown, the ball is relayed—sizzled in and snapped back— to the pitcher's glove.

Its own sound.

A pause, then a pitch follows.

*****

Joe has more of Baseball in Today's Time—without the longing tones of nostalgia—to pass along to Jim. Looking toward the fog in Jim's deep-set eyes, Joe announces that the senior league is where rookies learn how to play baseball—all over again—with the mind and body of a 50-,

60-, and 70-something, instead of a 20-, 30-, or 40-year-old player. Jim's adding it all up. Using his hands, he counts the decades in the beats on his quads.

"See Dick Giberti, the tall guy, as tan as a farmer, on the mound now?" Joe asks.

"Yeah, I think he's a wait and see guy. He's not buying the *Potential Success* idea as a guarantee. I'll have to win him over. He doesn't strike me as the sentimental type."

"A captain in the dugout, a retired aerospace engineer; you can handle his East coast ways. Slick and Dano drive the practices and work the players into baseball shape—so they can run, with knees up, into the next game."

Intent on tilling the soil of Jim's undertaking, Joe steers the rookie around the next bend that he doesn't see coming. Joe takes the pewter out and takes a sip, followed by another. "When you hit against Jesse Bower, you might as well bat righthanded. Lefty to lefty, his curve jumps inside to outside and is almost unhittable. Don't let your ego about your batting average or any statistics drag you down."

Joseph Lind starts off the dialogue in a manner to revive Jim's sunken spirits. "What did you hit in the 30-plus league when you were in your 40s?"

"The website hasn't recorded those years. But I'd say, in the .200s," Jim answers. No magic .300s.

"What did you hit in the 40-plus World Series games?"

Jim's eyes widen in spite of the tape and gauze. "In 12 games in two years, .316, .333, four singles, two doubles, a triple, a home run, a save, and a bunch of walks. That's what I am hoping to build on. The question is: how long will it take?"

"Uh, saves aren't hits,' Joe comments as if studying his notes. 'A triple, really?

Acting with a slanted pose, "I nearly needed oxygen after that one," Jim grimaces.

"At 44?

"I smoked back then. I quit soon after." Then, Jim strikes a steadier posture, like the staff of a capital I. You might say baseball saved my life."

"Okay, okay, you found your stride in your own age group. Some guys hit .500 in those games. You can't brag any more now that you're a player again. Bragging is for the retired."

"I'm kind of edgy, Joe. Anything left in that flask?"

"Do you want a shot?"

"Hand it over." Jim unscrews the top and raises it to his nose. He inhales the fragrances of cherries and grain. He shivers, "no" and hands it back to Joe, who holds it up to his eye. He pauses for a moment, making sounds while no words come out, turns the pewter upside down on his mouth and drains it.

Jim is staring at Joe. He flashes his angry eyes towards him. "Put the flask away, Joe. Before it kills you."

Like a quick-handed card dealer, Joe smuggles the flask into his pocket.

Joe's on a mission. His concern for his own health has escaped him. "Don't feel defeated before you start, but it may take you a few years to play full time in this league. They have players in their 40s. You're almost 60."

"Yes, but there are players my age and older. Look at Lowell Stalbaum, Geno Soldate, Slick Giberti, and others," Jim says.

"Remember, you've had a 12-year lay-off. A lot of these players have rarely missed a game." Joe stops talking and looks down at the rookie's new black Nike shoes. "Can you still run?"

"Yeah, on a dirt and grass field wearing cleats. Baseball fields are the only places I run. Home to first. Third to home."

"Long may you take a walk. Remember what Tim Hannan says: '"Baseball is a humbling game."'"

"Because there will be slumps. When you can't hit anything but a beachball, take a batting lesson from Hinkle at his backyard batting cage. He'll straighten you out. David Smith showed up there for 20 years. He never played baseball before that. Back then, he had many sub-.200 years. Now he's a bat to reckon with in the REBL."

"Where is his batting cage?"

"Oh, you'll catch a breath in the setting. It sits in the middle of a quiet, hilly neighborhood. You park your truck on a slant as steep as Potrero Hill in The City or Elizabeth Way in San Rafael. But the backyard is as flat as a tennis court. It sports a green carpet of turf, home plate, and a pitching machine that flings fastballs up to 60 MPH. It's covered in fishing nets, instead of this wire we're looking through in the dugout. You can see the backdrop of hilltops and hear the wind breathing in the trees, whispering—'focus,' and 'swing away.'"

"I won't feel trapped in a web? Okay, I'll give it a go."

"Do it, Jim," Joe says, pushing Jim's glove shoulder, "before the slump demons start talking back at you. You're a rookie without a batting average. Spring still follows even the harshest of winters. Nowhere to go but up. Nobody knows you except Dano and few others from your '90s stint."

Joe turns his body toward the action on the other side of the mesh. "Look out there. What do you see?"

"Burgandy hats, green, a lot of arms and legs moving around and having fun."

"Do you see the screen mesh?"

"How couldn't I?"

"But you didn't before I asked, right? To borrow one of Jim Brown's signature statements, 'that's what I'm talking about,' that's what I'm talking about. The mesh stands for the injustice of downbeat reasoning that hijacks your spirit. Worse, it's the analytic lines of the doubters and critics—both your own and those who would rather talk than play. The mesh is the grid of modern life, yes, but it's more than that. It's the wired brain of resistance, the dark web of doubt. Bias jurors of your trials on the baseball field deliberate for weeks on end in its cold mesh. Your job is to retain your fervor. Let the statistics be and the hits fall where they may."

"Okay, coach, got it." Now Jim becomes the silent one. He drums on the wooden bench as he contemplates the afternoon.

Joe's face lowers for a pause; his squinted creases of joy sketch lines across his face. He slinks over to Jim, approaching a serious undertone, "Watch out for Otto. He's a Jekyll and Hyde: he's both the gladdest hand and the sourest perspective on the field.

20

"Otto wants to steal your happiness, the joy you have carried since the early years of dreaming and playing real baseball. He's jealous of your home run. And proud of your failures. Remember, having success among failures is part of the game. It can never be stolen. And it won't be tainted, either. It *will* be challenged, however. Are you up to the challenge?"

"Fastballs and curves, sure. I can't wait to take the field again. Even driving to and from the park makes for a good day. I'm ready to play."

Remember, as Hinkle would say with that infectious Irish tenor of his, "'If you hit .300, you are failing 70% of the time. And that will get you in the Hall of Fame.'"

Lastly, Joe points through a large window of diamonds in the crisscrossed mesh, toward Dano.

"Yeah, I like Dano, too." Jim says,

Joe says, "Like Hinkle, he's all over the field. Ain't no position he hasn't played. Now *he's* a guy who stands in the complexity of his emotions."

"I relax around Dano," Jim says. "There is nothing perfect or neat about him. He just wants to play smart baseball."

"Dano's groomed by the six feet of musky air, humidified by sweat and beaded brow, and shaped by the spiraling dust of hundreds of ballfields," Joe says.

"He's a brother. I can tell already; he's the legal counsel when it comes to talking to the umpires on this team," Jim says.

"The Maverick." Joe, red-faced, pointing his index finger against his temple, adds a trance-like, spooky voice reminiscent of Peter Lorre in

Casablanca: "he's got the baseball rulebook tattooed on his extra-inning brain."

Joe's eyes and the rookie's ears lend their logics back to the field's music that plays on the chain-link fence's other side. Practice and its variations of sound absorb their scattered contemplations. Joe the sage, and Jim, the returning student. Old friends on a park bench. "Remember," Joe says, "the ball doesn't always move in a straight line. Straight lines are for computer games and lonely Nevada highways."

*****

Sunday morning baseball. Nine A.M. The dugout lies empty in the persistent sun, where currents of Pacific air stir up leftovers of infield dust. Beyond the further outfield fence, a young man drives a motorized chair topped with a little orange flag. He stops and waves to the trio of players standing 'round the on-deck circle. Wearing a black-as-mud cabernet Oaks jersey and Barry Bonds' number 25, he motors to the fountain. Parks next to the dugout. "You guys ready to play today? I'm Dano's adopted brother—my name's Coach Jeff. Around the house, we call Dano 'Running Bear.' I have cerebral palsy, so I get to drive this cart. This year's going to be fun. I don't know where we're going, but it's not over the hill."

Vista desde la Primera Base

Un buen lugar para parar,
platicar con jugadores,
tratar con asuntos de béisbol,
y atrapar una estrella fugaz.

Jugadores se esfuerzan por aterrizar aquí a salvo
antes de que llegue la pelota.
Se avientan, saltan, o se deslizan para llegar aquí primero.

Primera base.
Un lugar al cual jugadores corren
y abandonan,
anhelando volver en tardes breves de verano
en sus labores por las bases.

Un jugador se aleja de la base.
Pasos de un gato en cacería—izquierda sobre derecha, un salto

o calamidad,
y una inmersión de nuevo en el polvo.

Así funciona la inspiración,
años después de su chispa.

Revolvemos por primera base,
mirando momentos disolver en el pasado—

hablamos de forma ruda o trivial,
algunos poquito, algunos mucho—

y platicamos de las cosas sencillas.

First Base Vista

A good place to stand,
talk to players,
take care of baseball business,
and catch a shooting star.

Players strive to land here safe
before the ball arrives.
They dig, leap, or slide to get here first.

First base.
A place players run to
and abandon,
longing to return on brief summer afternoons
on their slogs around the bases.

A player leads away from the bag.
Cat-hunting steps, left over right, a leap

or disaster,
and a dive back into the dust.

Kind of how inspiration works,
years after its spark.

We shuffle around first base,
watching moments dissolve into the past—

rough talk, slim talk,
some a little, some a lot—

and speak of simple things.

Lightning Strikes and Wood Bats

Baseball creates its own language of simile and metaphor: the seeing-eye hit, the bleeder, the blooper, and the bomb, to name four. In the REBL, plays are boiled down to the slightest detail. That's where a new language of perception develops. Occasionally, the player needs to take a long walk with a few of his friends and say something new about what he sees.

Hot day on the diamond, any-town-in-the-world, Oaks down by three. Slick marches to the mound and warms up to relieve the starter. As he readies for the pitch, the ball lies loosely in his fingers as would a horse's reins in full gallop. Strike one. He's cutting the diamond again, shaving the plate.

Some call senior baseball a retirement gig. Slick isn't retired; he runs the Oaks' home-and-road show every day until the season's ended and the fields lie dormant for the crows.

Slick pitches. Fly ball tails toward the line; Dr. David Smith, the Oaks right fielder they call Smooth, styles the basket catch and runs the shortest path to the ball. He glides across the grass, flipping his glove out. In it, the ball lands. *Pop*. A pediatrician by profession—furrow-browed and bearded like Freud—he brings his study to the outfield and has the "cottonest" hands in the league.

The next hit screams past Smooth and rolls down the line. Digging for his life, the batter slides into second. Blue hollers, "Safe!" Quick dust torrents exit the infield as if the horses were stampeding in all directions. Before every pitch, Slick glares and checks the runner; his eyes stretch from under his cap to second base. After ball one and strike one, Slick snags the catcher's throw back and leans in for the sign. Quick as a tug on the horse's reins, he steps off the slab, pivots, and fires a dart to the second baseman. "Out." A wake-up call for drama stored in the player's soul. The batter hurries, head down, across the diamond. The Greek chorus in the dugout grumbles. Picked off. Getting fired while the small town watches.

Teammates don't answer the proverbial question, "Why play baseball at 60?" Most have played the game for decades with their fathers, families, and friends. They see plenty of reasons to stop but do not. They know that paying attention and focusing on the moment at hand—like when the pitch is thrown, or the ground ball is coming right at you—is the best remedy for the risks of playing baseball.

*****

Grey smoke drifts ever so slowly like a monster storm sneaking into the city. Outside the gates of G. Park, past the short wall where a small balding man watches time escape in the four corners, the latest war—too many to count—drags on with no end in sight. The recession deepens, and foreclosures become the big story. Real estate values drop more certain than stones crumbling off the last ledge of boom time. One more glad tiding arrives early morning in a drought year.

Fire! The northern state of California burns like no time in recorded history. Lake, Mendocino, Napa, and Sonoma Counties took on one too many lightning strikes last night. Hundreds of fires on the rampage. What hovers over the field is smoke, sliding shut like elaborate doors in the asthmatic sky to summer's ever-blue dome. To the north, the blue Mayacamas Mountains obscure as the moons drops into a sea of midnight; to the east, one can't see the forest on Sonoma Mountain, the vineyard across the road, or the horses and Black Angus on the ranches. A car in the next lane vanishes on a smoke-havoc road. In the rearview mirror, forest sightings have bid farewell. And reappear as a burnt-ugly wilderness. Somewhere, a place flourishes without fires. Perhaps the ocean at sundown. Or in the hearts and desires of a few Oaks who, for an hour or so, turn a blind eye to the sad facts. Sunset exists here and players find refuge without fires at G. Park under the smoke's grotesque attendance.

The few Oaks bring bats, gloves, and baseballs by the bucketload to the field that lies in shifting rose-glow light. Guys compete with the fire, but the heavy fallout in the air weighs them down. The Oaks run flies down on the right field grass just under today's blistered clouds. They work on the basics. Watch the ball hit the glove. Line drives make fielders run to the white lines. A shoelace catch sends up a collective cheer. A bomb struck over a player's head turns him around enough to see his number, 35; his outstretched gloved hand reaches for the ball before meeting this side of the outfield fence with hands up.

Let go of that fence wire, the teachers say. That's our outer limit. After the ball flies over it, you can't do anything about it. When it's gone, it's gone forever.

Some balls pop out of gloves; others fall untouched. Teammates holler and run the play over and over till they get happy or, when they are not relaxed, try to relax. Slick yells, "Remember the basics. Squeeze the ball in your glove. It's the best edge against dropping it." Back paddling, the rookie's feet tangle up; he drops himself and falls on his tailbone but holds on to the ball. No cheers for that.

He walks back to the end of the line and Otto, that guy Joe warned him about, slaps him on the back. "What's a matter, did you tie yourself into a knot that you couldn't untie?"

Some days in the outfield, guys don't talk much; they watch, run, and count. In the seamless smoke, the few count till their number comes up. "Three, you're up next." "Three" chases down a lateral fly. His legs running ahead of his hat get him there on time. His glove reaches for the setting sun and the ball finds it. Waves of cheers for that one.

The visitor, Little Eddie, the Oaks' biggest fan, sits on a short wall's ledge watching the Oaks practice. Eddie, nearly ninety years old, boasts a thick German accent. Eddie greets Dano—a mannish, jovial, rumbling bear of a man—as he arrives for practice at three o'clock sharp. Dano, a friend of anyone who loves baseball, walks through the smoke and pats Eddie on the shoulder. He leans into the gentle man, and with a volume of 10 and says, "Thank you for coming out to see the Oaks play." Eddie's head tilts as he answers in a whisper, "I like to watch baseball. You guys are pretty good, too."

Wood bats sound loudly around the REBL. A regular nickelodeon of sounds: a flash of light, clean crack, light thud, supersonic echo, thin tick, fat boom, pop, muddled crack, breaking bat. Even a mockingbird would have a difficult time with that cacophony.

Practice on an ordinary Wednesday. No metal bats allowed. Dano crows, "It's a wood bat league." Slick is throwing batting practice. Tall, stocky, and with a long reach-back, he exploits the hitters' weaknesses. He leans back and fires a half dozen pitches low on the inside corner. The

30

rookie's sluggish bat swings as if underwater. The flailing bat blurs the tranquility of stars in his eyes. Next pitch. Not a thud breaks the silence, only the grating dissonance of two Steller's jays squabbling in some invisible tree.

"Wake up," Dano yells from the dugout. "It goes farther when you see it." Slick adds, "Make music with your bat, Jim." The rookie sends a seed over second. Slick barks and fires one down the middle, "When it looks like a grapefruit, it fries like an egg." Crack. Zing.

Jim turns and strides back to the dugout. His spine is as straight as the spine of the capital L. He's feeling his Love for the game, enough to reveal a partially eclipsed smile. He's talking to himself. "Glad I hit that last one."

In a field as large as G. Park, standing precisely in the path of Jim's footsteps, Otto—hardwired to dim, diminish, and contain—plants his feet so Jim has to walk around him. Otto says, "What's a matter Rookie, no home runs today?"

Jim replies in stride and doesn't look back. He takes the available outside lane, "I'm just trying to make contact." What he wanted to say was, "and don't bother me." However, the grand baseball day melted the mesh of angry constraint. He is riding the lift from those last swings, listening to the pop in the bat on the hit to centerfield.

Still talking to himself, he returns to the dugout to retrieve his glove. Loops back onto the field to shag flies.

In his movement from the dugout to the field, he learned something. To the invisible ears that hear he says, "It takes courage to become a hitter. If you don't have courage, you will starve but for the kindness of devils."

31

Jim's on the field now, pounding his glove, readying for the chase of a few flies. He's looking into the batter in the on-deck circle. He doesn't see him from 250 feet away. He sees a 10-year-old in flannels on the field at Rancho Nicasio in late 50s Marin County. In the league championship game. T&B is down by nearly 10 runs. It's the bottom of the last inning—the sixth. T&B's bats are striking it rich and the other team sags with a suddenly erratic pitcher. T&B is scoring runs. Three or four by now. The bench and the fans awaken with golden throats and silver bells. Jim's leaving the on-deck circle for the one place he dreads. Home plate. Two outs. Two on. Amplified bells in the stands ringing the sounds of freedom and victory. Coach John Brookman hollers, "You can hit it as well as anyone. Go on and do it." Next pitch, Jim swings and grounds to third. He takes off. Maybe he'll beat the throw.

The ball arrives first. The season ends. Though they rang last year and this, the bells stopped. They didn't ring again until he stood in the batter's box at ASU. Here, at crack of the bat, Jim's chasing a fly that sticks in his glove, hurls it to David Smith, who with arms out and glove steady as a statue, stands at the ready in short right field.

Over the commotion, Jim Brown yells, "That's what I'm talking about."

As time will often prove, living in present time creates a victory over past time—and its haunting failures.

32

Cuánto Más Ruidoso Sea el Cuero,
Mejor el Lanzamiento

Golpea del bate sonando como la ruptura de un árbol talado,
rebota como una ardilla por el pasto, pega la tierra
donde cualquier cosa puede pasar,
y se levanta al hueco del guante del jardinero.

El campocorto poda el huerto en las manos, encuentra la pelota de fruta
que acaba de exprimir.
Su sombra se expande—aumenta mientras miembros más largos estiran.
Lanza una a primera base,
tan derecho como una ruta de vuelo de un carpintero.

Cada jugador arroja una pelota diferente.
Algunos vuelan como los Patos Cucharón Norteños—
en todas las direcciones.

Cuando llega zarpando, míralo pasar rápido con los ojos fascinados,
y perderé el vistazo para atrapar la maldita cosa del aire.

Un salto en vano mientras la pelota gira sobre mi guante
estirado como un árbol.
Como gansos llamando a través de una ventisca,
la pelota se evapora en la capa marina.

Cada jugador arroja una pelota diferente—a primera base.
Algunos se sumergen como fochas—
y con la rodilla hacia abajo,
lancearé el arco del lanzamiento con la mano de trampero,
donde el cielo reflejado del lago muestra el arco iris capturado.

Sigo de rodillas; pelota en guante. Dios mío,
¿no me lanzas otra?

Cada jugador arroja una pelota diferente.
Cuanto más ruidoso sea el cuero, mejor el lanzamiento.

Lounder the Leather, Better the Throw

It cracks off the bat sounding like the split of a stricken tree,
bounces like a squirrel across the grass, hits dirt
where anything can happen,
and kicks into the hollow of fielder's glove.

The shortstop prunes the orchard in his hands, finds the ball of fruit
he has just squeezed.
His shadow expands—heightens as longer limbs stretch.
He slings one over to the first baseman,
straight as a carpenter's snapline.

Every player throws a different ball.
Some fly like northern shovelers—in all directions.

When it sails in, watch it streak,
with eyes held in fascination,
and I'll lose the glimpse it takes to snag the darn thing from the air.

A vain leap as the ball wheels over my tree-stretched glove.
Like geese calling through a fog,
the ball evaporates in the marine layer.

Every player throws a different ball—to first base.
Some dive like coots—
and with knee down,
I'll spear the arc of the throw with my trapper's hand,
where the pond's reflected sky illustrates the netted rainbow.

I'm still on my knees; ball in mitt. Oh lord, will you toss me another?

Every player throws a different ball.
The louder the leather, the better the throw.

Ninguna a la línea de base, ruego,
justo en el sendero del corredor. Si lo haces, tendré que salir
y engancharla sin ser pisoteado.

Y girar y robarle al oso de pardo, quien—disparándose con boca abierta,
fosas nasales ardientes, y ojos de binoculares, curvando su espina para
estar fuera del alcance del guante—

huele y sabe, con la hambruna de un cazador, la base que he reclamado
para celebrar.

*****

Por un momento claro y breve del pasado,
la pelota nunca se detuvo.
Giró justo de la mano—una botella del estante—como una copa dorada
de vino reserva en un terremoto,
liberado de la rigidez del tiempo.

Y se cayó. Y finalmente se paró.
El error pavoroso. La mancha sobre el suelo de tierra.

Y el oso pardo, el entrenador de primera base, y el león llamado Blue—en
vez de mi equipo—tomaron el vino en primera base.

Not to the baseline, I plead,
smack in the path of the runner. If you do, I'll have to step out
and hook it without getting trampled.

And spin and swipe-tag the grizzly barreling by, who—
with mouth agape, nostrils blazing, and binocular'd eyes,
curving his spine to dodge the glove's reach—

smells and tastes, with a hunter's famine, the bag I've staked
for celebration.

*****

In one clear and brief moment from the past,
the ball never stopped.
It rolled right out of my hand—a bottle off a rack—
like some golden goblet of cellared wine in an earthquake,
freed from the rigidity of time.

And dropped. And lastly it stopped.
The dreaded error. A stain on earth's dirt floor.

And the grizzly, the first base coach, and the lion named Blue
—instead of my team—drank the wine at first base.

Even organic farmers have time for Sunday baseball

Ladd Miyasaki—Sonoma, California

Boomtime again. Golis Park or G. Park, as the players call it, is a vast parcel of wine country real estate. Its clay—crushed brick, bad-hop infield, and miles of bluegrass outfield—is provided by volunteers and the withered budget of the city of Rohnert Park. Not many home runs fly out of G. Park. Not by 60-year-olds anyway. Although former San Francisco Giant Rich Murray, who does look giant-like and towers over most players, hit one out of G. Park where few hit home runs. Dead center is 385 feet away. His affection for the game allows us to witness the movements of jubilation at work.

Jim is used to looking at a computer every day and sometimes all night. Now, as a right fielder, he watches the batter swing, sees a grain of rice 300 feet away, runs a few steps toward it—as the ball rushes through light and shadows faster than a lightning strike—arriving so close, so quickly. Finishing the catch, his eyes follow it into his glove pocket. Voices spring up from the field. He flings the ball back to the cut-off man. This is happiness.[vi] When the play is made, the air sweetens. No time to dwell. Next pitch.

An ocean breeze hurries in from right field most afternoons while the sun camps out on the pitcher's shoulder and blinds the hitter. Ruts outline the infield. One off-weekend while the team slept in, Slick, Dano, and Cookie dug up the mound and the batters' boxes, buried bricks in the holes, and covered them over with clay. Nothing worse than throwing a pitch and landing in a rut that turns into a hole.

Smooth says, "Ralph's the one guy on the team who dirties his uniform before a game." Ralph, missing teeth and the Oaks' catcher—a throwback from a bygone era—slides headfirst into the game. Dust flies. Safe. Where he stands, dirt descends like soot from a chimney sweep. In the fall, his twenty-nine stolen bases will lead the team that plays a twenty-game season. Rarely does a player see Ralph thrown out when Blue sees the tag in front of his head with both eyes on the ball. Ralph's a two-sided coin; his vocalness behind the plate irritates the infielders, like a parasite does an oyster, and makes them play better. Sometimes, his mask flies off and we hear the grunt when he throws runners out, 2-6 for scorekeepers. Off their feet and back to the dugout.

After practice, Eddie waves goodbye as the few wander to their backyard parties and barbeques. In the smoke, Eddie sits and flags down David Smith, who speaks German. The Oaks see 4' 9" Eddie perching on the short wall by the threshold to G. Park every day. He sits as the outside looks in, while the honeybees collect pollen from baby blue rosemary blooms. He can be viewed as an old man, a stranger from afar, except by those who live somewhat afar in their own right. May we embrace his strength as well as his fragility, and value his need to glean hellos from the ballplayers who remind him that he exists at all.

And when the parking lot empties, he communes with precious time in the burnt red sun. Then, he pulls his slouch hat down, lifts the cane off his idle arm, and places it firmly on the concrete ground. Between the few stones strewn across like the first evening stars, he steps lightly and drifts out of the park—a man filled to the brim with the Sunday afternoon `

Eight players from the Sutter Home Classics, a tough-nut team from Napa, walk past little Eddie one spring morning. One outfielder short, Napa asks Slick to loan them an Oaks' player. They don't call him Slick for nothing. Slick and Dano veto that idea real quick. Rules say eight is enough to play in the REBL, so play begins at ten sharp.

A run here, a run there, the Oaks score, and Napa's bats get hot. On a line drive between first and second base, the rookie, standing even with the bag, cuts right at the wallop. His arm's stretched out for the grab, but he doesn't see the ball's spin as it arcs away. It hits the toe, the hard spine at the woven edge of his mitt, and ricochets away to freedom. The field withers with the music of deflation. The air is let out of the balloon. Moans of the team fall into a deafening silence. What did Joe say about the ball not moving in a straight line?

The Oak's catcher, Ralph, who smells like he had bacon and eggs, for breakfast, loves dirt, sweat, and playing in the fate of the wild card. He takes a foul tip off his hand, hits the ground, forgets the pain of hammered bone, and fires the ball back. He calls a breaking ball in the dirt. Base hit to center. The streets are loaded with Classics.

Ralph tames the wolf mob from themselves. Mask off. Fire rolls from Ralph's mouth. Nearly black patches of sweat appear on the Oaks' blood red uniforms. "Time, Blue." Ralph motors to the mound and looks Big Al in the eye. Al shuffles, scrapes his cleats, looks down to the infinity beneath the mound. Sweat has popped across his forehead like forgotten rain drops and he has clearly lost his poise. Ralph whispers a newly discovered compassion, "That last guy got lucky—focus down and in, and throw strikes on his hands." The rookie and Tim McGaw eavesdrop a

41

half-step closer. Then Ralph adds, "Al, are you okay, can you see straight?" Al wobbles but anchors his legs and nods. "I'm good." Ralph, head turning to all evident players, surveys the field and, with finger pointed to his temple, bellows to the entire cast as they quicken to their positions, "Focus."

Baseball's small steps amplify into wide leaps. The rookie jogs to his spot anchoring the first base corner. On his way, out of nowhere in particular, a faint scent of caramelly cure revives the edgy air. The sounds of infield chatter follow him like murmuring crows. He feels more at home alongside the bag than watching the landscape blur while running around in the outfield. Since his bat hasn't exactly caught fire today, and he still hasn't called Hinkle, first base has become his passion.

Mask on. Ralph roars, "Corners in." The infielders' springs become coiled to strike. On bended knees, the rookie first baseman and third baseman, McGaw, creep past the edge of the infield grass, staring at the batter. A one-hopper to first, the runner on third breaks for home; the rookie gloves the baseball and throws—high to the plate. High enough that Ralph leaves his feet. In the air, he looks less a wild boar, more a crazed scientist. He's part steel worker and part bullfighter and—with the runner bearing down on him—sees only the ball. It and the runner arrive, and the players collide. On the equivalent spot where his quick tag was to lunge for sliding spikes, Ralph crashes to the dirt with the ball stuck in his catcher's mitt. A twisted heap, eyes flickering like strobe lights, he creaks and growls awake. Dano, nicknamed Running Bear for such occasions, has called Blue out. A conference of eight players, managers, and umpires darken home plate with shadows. A full-throated Bear in the middle.

With barrel chest and obsessive lust for the game, Dano looks a lot like the Babe, though not as tall. More the height of Yogi than the Babe, he's a born catcher. If a runner plows into Running Bear, he hits a dense mass of bone and skull. Dano informs Blue, "The guy ran over my catcher, and the rule book says he's out of the game." Blue heard Dano, as did the folks at church in downtown Cotati. Classics' roster falls to seven. Dano presses: "The rule book says no team can play with seven players."

Oaks win by a forfeit. Ralph shrugs off toward the dugout, telling both teams, "I'm okay, I'm okay." He grabs some pine next to his daughter, Ashley. The Oaks on the bench change into street shoes. The stench of sour socks—like the month-old chunk of Limburger that high schoolers smuggled under the backseat of a grouchy neighbor's car—fouls the light air that made wood and leather once smell sweet. Coach Jeff, sitting at the end of the dugout, says, "You're gonna feel it tomorrow." Ralph wonders, "Why'd the guy run into me?" Running Bear saunters by, "Because you can't figure out what you can't figure out."

Ashley sprinkles joy around the dugout and the rookie dubs her "Muse." With curly locks flopping, she jumps up at Slick—instead of her father, Ralph— "Do we have to go home already?" A dancer in the making, she cartwheels on the base line, twirling her arms like batons.

Jim goes through the ritual of unlacing his spikes, and wrapping his glove, with a belt and three baseballs squeezed inside to form its pocket. Bewildered and dirty in a good way, he is relieved that he didn't come up to bat with the game on the line. He's resolving that folding of the metaphoric cards by plotting to call Hinkle.

43

Meanwhile, Otto, the laziest guy on either team, who walks like he's wearing a scarlet cape rather than an Oaks uniform, breezes through the dugout and sits next to Jim. The scent of Old Spice arrives soon after. He looks kind of like Joe but is medium-tall rather than extra-large tall. His hair is dyed a shoe polish black that blots on his forehead whenever he sweats—he wears a clownish game face— he's stuck grinning as if his face is made of plastic. Really, no matter what is happening, he wears a grin as affixed as a kiosk in an empty parking lot. It gets to be unnerving to most everybody and to the umpires as well.

But that's Otto. He wears no number on his back. Meant figuratively as well, every number in the ballpark today is grander. Otto stares at Jim's black leather A2000 with the three baseballs in the pocket. His plastic smile disappears; the duel is about to begin.

"What are you doing there?" Otto asks.

"Oh, I call it glove love," Jim answers. "You know, molding the pocket."

Jim knows immediately he has played the wrong card. Honesty doesn't work with a guy like Otto. He watches Otto take the needle from his own mouth in an effort to jab it into Jim's spirit.

"So, you're the guy taking all the baseballs home! Ha, ha, followed by ha, ha, ha."

Jim lies to him and fires back. "I showed up my first day with 10 baseballs, asshole, so, shut the fuck up."

He doesn't want to tell the long story: that Slick and Dano had given him the green light to bring home a few baseballs for practice. He wants to stand up in a hurry, get this over with, and bid Otto his farewell.

But Otto stands up first, the corners of his mouth rising in his smiley Ken Doll face.

"See you at practice," he says. "Be sure to bring that glove love with you next time. Ha ha, followed by ha, ha, ha, ha!" Then he fades permanently into the pathological grid he fell from.

Ralph and the team roam past Eddie. Players are still stunned by the play that ended the game. One of the Classics stops by Eddie's ledge to ask him a question with the obvious answer. "Did you play baseball in Germany?"

"No," he answers, eyes straight ahead through gathered clouds of soft age, and with a spine like a stack of rocks, "we didn't play baseball. We played work. I worked when I lived in Germany."

"Even as a kid?"

"Yeah, that's why I lived so long. Hard work. I'm going to be ninety next year."

Off the field now, Ashley joins the group. "I play ball, too, you know, at my school. Besides dancing, I mean. My teacher told me that half of everyone in the world's heard the crack of a bat."

Eddie perks up from his 30-second siesta, the kind of snooze you have when you're approaching your 90th birthday. "I want somebody to listen to me," he pleads. Most of the players adjourn but Smith and Lenehan remain. After a pause, they listen up. "I played soccer in Germany. I wasn't strong, but I was quick."

Nothing exists but Eddie and the universe of his harvested life.

Béisbol Dentro y Fuera del Tiempo

Nos despertamos al amanecer.
Tenemos que llegar; el diamante frío no espera a nadie.
La ciudad empapada de lluvia previene que juguemos,
pero aun así encontramos el campo bajo la capa de neblina.

Hierba cortada, tierra barrida, agua preciosa,
día silencioso, un motor suena una milla de distancia—nada me molesta.
Nada más que
bates de béisbol de ceniza y arce estirando por la pelota.
Negro, café, dorado, rojo, plateado, azul, y
mitad y mitad.

Bienvenido a béisbol. Bienvenido a la vida.
No hay ningún 360 millón que haga subir el precio.
Pagamos para jugar.

Piernas caminan penosamente en hierba del cuadro, guantes
hacia fuera, encontrando su equilibrio hasta la tarde.

La bola alta—arqueándose bajo la bandada de gansos de nieve,
una cápsula espacial cayéndose del cielo del jardín—
se deja caer en la mano de un jardinero, la flor del loto, y el guante.

Bienvenido a béisbol. Bienvenido a la vida.
El cuero y la respiración pesada impregnan
el apretón profundo de la captura.
Aplaude el sudor y celebra la tierra empinada.

Juega por un tiempo corto o por treinta años,
o por toda la vida, o—si cuentas volviendo a cero—
todas las edades.

Aún si nunca jugabas, puedes aprender.
Tengo la prueba. Tengo nombres.

Baseball In and Out of Time

Wake at daybreak.
Gotta get there; the cold diamond waits for no one.
Rain-drenched city precludes play,
but we find a way to the field layered under fog.

Mowed grass, raked dirt, precious water,
silent day, a motor sounds a mile away—no bother.
Nothing but
ash and maple bats reaching for the ball.
Black, brown, blond, red, silver, blue, and
half and half.

Welcome to baseball. Welcome to life.
Ain't no 360 million driving up the price.
We pay to play.

Legs traipsing on outfield grass, gloves drawing out,
feet digging under green, finding footing into afternoon.

The fly ball—arcing under the flock of snow geese,
a space capsule falling from the outfield sky—
drops into a fielder's hand, lotus, and glove.

Welcome to baseball. Welcome to life.
The leather and the heaving breath permeate
the deep squeeze of the catch.
Applaud the sweat and celebrate the steeped dirt.

Play for a short time or thirty years,
or a lifetime, or—if counting back to zero—
all ages in-between.

Even if you never played, you can learn.
I have proof. I have names.

Los novatos, los que toman su turno al bate—como inmigrantes
que llegan, el cambio de la guardia, y el líder del largo recorrido de
los gansos de nieve—
siempre son bienvenidos.

The rookies, the ones who take their turn at bat—like arriving
immigrants, the changing of the guards,
and the leader of the snow geese's long haul—
are always welcome.

Infield

The REBL umpires show up on Sundays like the players but exist in a different universe at times. Especially when the game is past the halfway mark, say the sixth inning on a hot day. Then the strike zone widens by two or sometimes three inches on the far side of the plate.

In the game, the crows argue louder in the batter's head than the crows in the trees when the umpire—the man called Blue—calls a poorly thrown pitch: "Strike three." When Blue breaks the silence that many eyes verify as wrong, it knocks the birds loose in the players' heads. All eyes fly into the void, zeroing in on Blue. I'm sure he feels a funeral in his brain. Because the anguished outcries in the Oaks dugout are rising fast. Blue's torment flows from the never-ending Steller blue jays' squawking from the dugout.

He yanks off his mask from his heap of black and grime, revealing puffy red cheeks and globular eyes that could drill stone and bore holes through the skulls of any baseball player and the few rare fans in attendance. A central part of the game, his words become law. Especially when he pulls off his mask. His expression erupts and changes from an O to X to "vexed" in a flash instant. He aims his forefinger toward the dugout and throws Otto out of the game. Otto has to miss the following week, per REBL rules. This place and time find the Greek chorus blowing up past volume 10 with added echo and reverb. The dugout wire mesh is sizzling, sparking, and popping off. And in that process, team spirit emerges within the conflict. Mass sympathy backs up Otto in a prolonged outcry. The grey wings stop flying. The sky ices over with a thick and blinding fog.

The rookie can't tell if Eddie's sleeping or bored with this scene, but his eyes are closed.

*****

A player in the heat of the moment will do anything to avoid strike three. Suspensions don't deter Slick and Dano. They get axed every season arguing calls, fighting for baseball justice. Justice is not a given. Even in senior baseball. But like the world outside, sometimes it is. Real justice is like having a switch hitter, with power, bat from both sides of the plate. Two sides to every story and both sides will be heard. In other words, a balanced scale of justice and impartiality.

Baseball has its appeal process, but its umpires are totalitarians, obviously. They will listen sometimes, but other times? Blue doesn't weigh the arguments except with another Blue. The call stands by what they see, hear, and sometimes a sixth sense comes into play. If the managers take over the game, anarchy will result. It can't be real baseball without a real human umpire. It's a good idea to greet them early in the game.

Otto slams his gear into his bag with all the care of a bank robber and escapes the field as the discourse continues. The unbroken grin finally quakes into a scowl. He's doesn't smile. His face freezes. In his teammate's eyes, he's captured in various postures, with a stunned and droopy face. The hunter becomes the hunted. A block of ice to put back into the freezer.

*****

Otto can't play in this week's game, but he can practice with the team per league rules. The swing and miss: a deafening silence for a hitter.

51

Exclamation point when the catcher's mitt booms. But a swing and broken bat? There's a spare around here somewhere. Otto doesn't have a backup bat. Slick carries 12. Dano, eight. Jim has three. He and Otto meet half-way between the plate and the dugout for the exchange of the broken for the hand-me-down. The gallery of fielders at practice lightens up. Eddie's hands, as small as sparrows, flutter, clap, and his eyes squinch as if to say, "wait—don't do that!"

But Jim did. And on the second pitch, Otto broke bat number two for today. On his way back to the dugout, he hands the broken bat, complete with the splintered jagged edge of a foot-long split along the handle back to Jim. "Not a very good bat. Where's you get it? That's two bats I got to buy tomorrow." Jim wanted to tell him that he had the label facing the pitcher and call him a dumbass, but he called on the deities of all colors and creeds to stop him. Jim sometimes says what he wants the other person to say to him. "Sorry, man."

There's no mesh, grid, or obstacles to look at, no sense of alienation when Jim's out on the field, practicing with his teammates. There's an equality, a harmony on the field, that rises above the petty facts, the provoking phantoms, and the grids of unreasonable reasoning. When the need for balance in an X, Y, Z, situation arrives, one of the players speaks up and says what he sees. Another player provides the response that fills the void. It doesn't matter from whom. The words, "sorry, man," had to come from Jim because the silence was deafening and Sisyphus's stone was getting heavier and was pushing him back down the hill.

Slick would disagree. He'd repeat one of his favorite axioms, "No sorrys and no tears in baseball, gentleman. It's that simple."

One more hot Wednesday afternoon, Dano—looking like the lone bear that ambles across Yosemite Valley—steers the mower on the outfield grass. The swirling smells of cut grass inundate the senses. He's oblivious to everything else. Teammates take batting practice. Fly ball ricochets off Dano's front tire. The Greek chorus shrieks a pithy alarm. A line shot zings over his head. Could have given him a dent or a haircut. Dano looms as large as granite Zeus under the elephant-grey sky while he mows the vast theater of outfield. Dano can't lift his arm over his head. A torn rotator cuff prohibits him from buckling on the catcher's gear, but with his bat, his shrewdness speaks in rocket line drives and high batting averages year after year. He's the essence of the game. "The closer, the better," he says. "Even if it hits me."

The sun crashes through smoke that weighs over 15,000 pounds times 1000. A thousand elephants graze in the sky. The sun's jagged rays filter down on Dano's squared face. He's tight mouthed, but behind his shades, he's always smiling. He stares dead ahead, steering the mower. He turns sideways and glances across the curtains of smoke at a player who shows up late. He waves. In and out of time, showing up is what matters most to Dano. A maestro at improvisation, he polishes the diamond, making it more radiant—set inside the vast symmetry of the ballpark— out of a pitted and parched casualty of economic meltdown and urban neglect.

Back at practice, Running Bear, a silver-toned fungo bat on his right shoulder, casts yet another serious shadow over home plate. "Corners in," he bellows. His bat knocks a hot-rock-shot-from-a-campfire to first to the rookie. "Wake up, infielders!" Thwacks a shot through third. "You got to get down." Infielders, gloves sniffing like bloodhounds for ground balls, pull up empty. "Get in front of it." Unless you're the fielder; then it's "Get behind it" to stop the ball from rolling into the outfield. "Get your butt out of your chair, Jim."

Neither passion nor obsession defines Dano. He carries that extra thermos of what seems like mythical soul in his equipment bag to this rough and tumble harbor-paradise, where teammates wrestle with younger versions of themselves. The effect is that he seasons the dedicated and makes them better ballplayers. He barks, knocks the ball around, and thrashes his fungo bat while players dart and cover infield ground. Dano The Motivator. As a result, he's Jim's best friend during the game. He swats one to the shortstop, who vacuums it up. "Get two." The second baseman, Wolverine, surrounds the flip from the shortstop, clasps his hands, pivots, and throws to first base. The ball skips five feet in front of Jim; it's out of reach and on the 95-degree day, the rookie becomes the frozen ice sculpture this time. Dano stops the action, bat at his side like a sword pointing to the earth, and implores the rookie first baseman, "I want you to make that play. If you got to come off the bag to catch it, jump out. Now, let's take five and get some water." The merciful Dano.

In the long summer drought, when smoke idles and lingers day and night like the growing numbers of unemployed, a job still must be done. Water. Rationed water, yes, but still, water! Rainbows appear in the small-world horizon. Slick sets up a Rainbird behind second base.

Alongside the dugout, the water fountain flows. Players line up. The line shuffles slowly while the water heaves swiftly. They drink, soaking heads and faces, in spite of the recursive joke in the fountain, "I peed here." Nothing said between gasps. Heavy breathing relays the story to the next in line. Wide, saturated eyes look up, ballooned. Ahh, the water tastes like champagne. Bloated faces drain. Hats off, they're lost in baseball cosmos. Thanks to Slick and Dano, the Jupiter and Zeus of G. Park's maintenance crew, a few cooler bodies drift toward the Rainbirds for even more. Rainbows.

Blues de Iritis

No puedo reírme, correr,
dar un paso rápido, leer, dormir,
o arrastrar la mano por el carbón flotante en el ojo.
Si estornudo, cangrejos echados en agua hirviente
me rascarán bajo los párpados.

Refrescan el camino; aprieto el frasco de gotas oculares
por la carga del cubo
por el día de levantar piedras.

Escucho cuando es incómodo
ver a través de los flotadores, las manchas de células inflamadas, y
pedacitos rotos de tiza negra, circulando el ojo como derrotan las alas de
un grupo de cuervos.
El sonido aumenta de graznidos y gorgoteos.
El cuerpo alivia la mente
durante el fildeo de la pelota.

Ida y vuelta al banco,
vierto una remedia de gotas lácteas.
Más que brillante, pero un rescate quizás esté en mi próximo batazo.

¿Requiere alguien en este equipo los ojos ebúrneos,
para enfriar el jabalí en el incendio forestal
bajo el hechizo de esteroides?

Paisajes sonorosos de voces y puños golpean guantes,
divirtiéndose en el diamante iridiscente de espejo azul.

Los ojos dilatados huyen el banquillo
para girar en las sombras.
Lentes de sol oscurecen el campo demasiado brillante
y estoy dando zancados al plato.
Empañado en un azul nube nimbo, el árbitro
murmura, "Jimmy, es hora de cantar una canción diferente
que esos blues de iritis. Strike tres."

Iritis Blues[vii]

Can't laugh, run,
turn a quick step, read, sleep,
or drag a hand across the floating coals in my eye.
If I sneeze,
crab claws, as if thrown in boiling water,
will scratch under my eye lid.

Cool the way; squeeze the vial of prednisone drops
by the bucketload
through the day of lifting stones.

I listen when it's awkward to see through the floaters, the smudges
of inflamed cells, and torn bits of black chalk, circling
the eye like trouncing wings of a treachery of ravens.
The rising sound of gurgling and croaks.
The body relieves the mind
when fielding the ground ball.

Back and forth to the bench,
I pour the remedy of milky drops.
Brighter than bright, but the rescue may lie in my next base hit.

Does anyone on this team require wintergreen eyes,
to cool the wild boar raging in the burning forest
under the spell of steroids?

Soundscapes of voices bark and fists pound gloves,
rollicking on the iridescent, blue-mirrored diamond.

Dilated eyes flee the dugout to
swing in the shadows.
Sunglasses darken the overbright field and I'm striding to the plate.
Fogged in a blue nimbus cloud, the umpire murmurs,
"Jimmy, it's time to sing a different song
than those iritis blues. Strike three."

Batting Practice

Slick and Dano run those "back-to-basics" practices, or clinics, that cover baseball's fundamentals. Their workouts set patterns and mold "baseball common sense" into alert brainwaves. On any given day, Dano runs the infield, and Slick leads the outfield and pitches some batting practice. Dano walks off and counts the base runner's primary and secondary steps for leading off base. Both teach completing the double play and the revolving order of fielders during a rundown. Both hit live infield popups with bats, and later, with bazooka-like pitching machine versions. Feet scoot and anchor under them, heads rising out of caps, arms up and bent, eyes following the quick flying, fast-falling ball, the size of milk opal through the paled sky.

On the mound, with his free hand pointing forward to the plate while standing by the pitcher's side, Slick, holding the ball in his right hand, mocks a real throw. He detains his arm in midair at the point along the arc of his motion, stopping at the point where the ball is released. "Know where to find your release point," he urges in that vital voice.

Dano, five feet before second base, runner at his side, slides feet first into the bag. The runner follows him after Dano jumps up and spins off the ground, his two feet landing at the same instant and his eyes fixed on the man's spikes, which cling to the bag. "Good slide," Dano boasts, clapping his hands and widening them, palms down. "You got low and parallel and prone in your upper body. Keeps you out of range from the high swipe tag." Jim, standing by, soaks it up. The school never closes with Slick and Dano. To learn the game, Jim has to show up and run those plays over and over again until the bad hops find his glove.

A catcher has nothing to do without a pitcher on the mound or, in some cases, sitting next to him on the bench. The ancient Zen axiom is fully illustrated, "It's not one, it's not two, it's one and two." The Oaks, loaded with pitchers, rely on Big Al Surges and Slick. Tall guys. Smart upstairs about the count, spin on a pitch, and location. Broad shoulders and long arms, always pitching from the back leg. Slick's pitch weighs like lead, a floating mine that breaks bats. The ball rarely leaves the infield. Big Al's got a pitch that looks buffalo-big and lazy, then rabbits down a hole. The hitter swings over a pitch that hits home plate. For the pitcher, a moment to savor; for the hitter, the mid-winter-wait-till-next-year's "at-bat."

Cookie, a third pitcher, looks as gritty as the cook on a 19th century wagon train with his big, rounded face and horseshoe mustache. Always concocting something, he's a studious observer of strategies like when to throw a curveball and when to waste a pitch out of the strike zone. For him, the mesh and the field are a little closer together; he's got both halves of the brain working side by side. I'm no neurologist, but Cookie is an educated man under his baseball gear. He's the Oaks' man behind-the-scenes; he closes—pitches the ninth sometimes.

Right fielder, Smooth, works from the plywood mound, covered in green felt, at former USF alumni and pitcher Rich Hinkle's backyard batting cage. If you hang out with Hinkle, a Cincinnati Reds draftee in 1967's summer of love, and lean into his few words, you're going to learn something about baseball.

Jim's looking at the mesh again. The rookie dreams because he doesn't have to worry about the numbers rising and falling in his batting average. He dreams of when he pitched back in the '90s and the years he threw to friends and to plywood catchers in rural yards. But he's not dreaming his life away. He sees the Oaks have lots of experienced pitchers.

McGaw throws a terse batting practice. He's all business on the mound with a tight-lipped and purposeful game face. Looking up with his eyes in the same place every pitch, he pulls his body into its core. The ball and glove meet out front in his two medium bent arms. He works with a slightly feverish aura that reveals his work ethic. No time to waste. Get the job done on time.

Patler's comeback train is on track to regain the hill. The Oak's train of boxcars is loaded with pitchers. So, the rookie left his pitching ambitions back at the station for a while; he had enough work to do showing up to play at all. His inspiration now is to become the best first baseman he can be and finish the rest of the season without an error. But something else happens. Confidence at home plate.

No talk of pitching in REBL is complete without Larry Hendrickson. The same year as Jim attempts his second rookie year in 2006, Larry pitches for his own team, the Silver Sox, in the more competitive 28 years-and-over-league, where he strikes out 100 batters and finishes the season with an ERA of 1.00 while winning 8 games. All that in a hitters' league that swings metal bats! That's enough to gain a rookie's hero status.

When Larry steps onto a baseball field, a few studious eyes follow his measured stride. Not overly tall, his motion is steady and compact rather than a flying delivery—he's quick armed with controlled power and can pitch a rumble through a barn door and fool a poker player with a flick of the wrist. He hides the ball so well that you can't pick it up in his hand; you don't see it until it's halfway to the plate.

Larry throws batting practice every Wednesday at G. Park. He carries his pitching screen across the diamond, then takes batters on a round-the-clock tour of the strike zone. He'll tip a few pitches to the hitter: "Curveball. Another curveball. Here comes a change-up. Good swing." With his sixth sense and 20 thousand roads of experience, he'll read the angle of a ball lasered back at him and duck behind the screen.

Slick says, "Make music with your bats, guys." Taking BP with Larry is like jamming with John Fogerty. A batting practice pitch sounds real good off the bat. Everyone within 300 feet hears the music. Some infielders hear the fuzz of the seams whizzing past their extended hands. The lazy fly ball sustains the note until landing beyond the outfielder's glove. Sometimes the big hit is launched, and the singing line drives boost the hitter's confidence.

But make no mistake: in games, Hendrickson will muscle up and hurl the pitch that screams past the hitter. The ball appears in the batter's eyes, unmoving like a comet in mid-flight, its red threads so tightly stitched, the batter could pick it out of the air by its seams—Official Ball stamped into the cowhide. It vanishes like a figment of the imagination. No sounds break the silence at that lonesome stop except for the thump of the glove, Blue's "strike," and the catcher shifting gears in his shoulder and grunting the ball back.

On the next pitch, a whisper of mound dirt kicks up as his left foot lands, pointing due south like an arrow toward the catcher. The batter swings over the curveball that twists his limbs and buckles his legs.[viii]

He finishes the pitch with throwing arm leaning down to the ground, parallel and mirroring slight crooks of his left leg. His spine and back become fixed at a 90-degree angle to the field; his face, stationary in purpose yet for a twitch of his greying mustache. Those certain eyes, following the spin of the ball into the place of no return, nod in agreement with Blue. "Strike."

But today is batting practice: the place where trust takes over, imaginary Blues call the game, and a swinging bat drums the backbeat to the music of the free world.

Confidence. Jim is hitting line drives to centerfield. He now knows what it feels like to hit a ball precisely between the borders of the bat. The sweet spot, the pop; they drive resistance and its companion despair far, far away.

.

Escapar de la Jaula de la Computadora
(una tarde de domingo en el estadio)

Esto es lo que un puñado de personas hace cuando
se da cuenta de que la escala del tiempo
está inclinada demasiado en favor del pasado;
jugamos en una liga de béisbol y esperamos un buen día
para jugar el mejor partido de nuestras vidas.
Algunos nos llaman "caballeros, tontos, ancianos solitarios;"
otros nos llaman artistas.

Los vacíos que tal vez tengamos por dentro
solamente pueden llenarse
por ese primer paso en el campo, una vez que abandonamos
el campo en sí después de un invierno largo y cubierto de hielo.
Retrocediendo en un trozo de luz verde, camaradería
entre amigos a veces distantes y otras veces más cercanos,
o aun hermanos, hemos llegado de vuelta.
Algunos se sienten lo suficientemente desesperados para decir que hemos
escapado de nuestras propias
jaulas colectivas
y de las telarañas que le han instalado los
sistemas operativos del siglo XXI a nuestra humanidad.

Escaping the Computer Cage
(on a Sunday afternoon at the ballpark)

This is what a handful of people do when we realize the scale of time
is tipped far in favor of the past;
we play in a baseball league and wait for a good day
to play the best game of our lives.
Some call us "gents, fools, lonely old men;" a few call us artists.

The vacancies we may have within us can only be filled
by that first step on the field, once leaving the very same field after a long
and ice-capped winter.
Stepping back onto a patch of green light, camaraderie among sometimes
distant and at other times closer friends, or even brothers, we have made
it back. Some feel desperate enough to say we have escaped our own
collective cages
and the webs that our 21st century operating systems have
downloaded upon humanity.

The Diamond Shifts

Sutter Home Classics roll in from Napa; the rematch is about to begin. All the Classics show up at Santa Rosa High School on the hottest day of the year—about 105 degrees at game time; the field lies in full August sunlight now. California wildfires have fallen asleep under tankers carrying dwindling water supplies, that is, until they awake with a vengeance down the road a year or two, when they'll be roaring back for more life and death chaos. A few Oaks players must have thought the game was called off because of the overwhelming heat: only nine, plus Dano, Slick, and Coach Jeff, show up. Otto has been nowhere to be found after he broke those two bats. The rookie may get his chance today. He greets an opposing player, "Hey."

Sutter's guy, smelling like this morning's Pinot Grigio, squelches rookie's longing for a handshake. Then his teammate alertly offers, "The only way you will beat us today is if we have seven players. And we have thirteen."

Ashley and her lucky locks bounce into the dugout. "Hum, hum, bumblebee buzz" is her hello to the team. "Are you ready to play today?" coach Jeff asks as the rookie lugs his gear in a black bag with *Oaks* emblazed in red. In severe heat, the Oaks will need a magic formula besides the water fountain. Coach Jeff's dad, Jon McGraw, plays right field today.[ix]

Dano, with bulging eyes, calls Jim over for a brief announcement. His voice booms decibels louder than talking side by side, more like a third base coach yelling at the runner to score.

67

"You're playing the whole game today, Jim. You can take the heat."

"I thrive in heat, Dano. I'm better moving through it than frying on the bench."

Dano thumps a hand on Jim's shoulder and barks, "Then warm up. You're the starting first baseman."

Ashley peers through the dugout screen at old, reliable Big Al Surges as he takes the hill. On the field, the heat distracts, plays tricks on concentration, and dilates flushed and bewildered faces. She studies the players serving up their infield and outfield throws. A ball flies through the air, hits the dirt, and rolls across the grass to the dugout. The team loosens knees and widens elbows under their black-billed hats. Their logo, a silver-stitched octagon-shaped letter O, embroidered over a Golden Bear, stands out against their claret-colored caps.

On the bench, sweat stings marble eyes. Wet towels leap from coolers and drape over bowed heads. Water—where from doth spring thy precious gift? Yellow jackets, in a frenzy, hover at the drinking spout as wasps ball up mud at the foot of the fountain. The trick is to gulp without sucking down a yellow jacket. Air—where doth waft thine ocean breeze? No beloved airstream cools the field. Tempers break on heat's short leash. Voices rise. Arguments without merit ensue. Heat comes out the winner. Each player knows—in his subconscious mind, where deep crevices of water and jagged rocks speak truth—that he has played better than this day. Poor play reveals time's abandonment of youth. Heat masquerades as a dazzling day; a desperation for shade enters the gates of the game.

Classics cruise and baseball scratches on. Ground ball to deep second near the bag. The leather hand slows time down, as quick feet race

68

to the ball. Wolverine's glove hits the dirt first. He spins and floors the gas petal. Ten feet before the base, the hitter's eyes and hat turn down and out. Jim's glove cocoons the throw from Wolverine before he wrist-flips a light toss to the pitcher.

Napa's quick-eyed lead-off hitter, a lefty with eyes bulging from anticipatory guile and unwavering bat, lines one off the bag at first base. Rookie's feet, like a gangster wearing cement shoes, freeze. A primitive thing occurs within the heart of a baseball player. Desire for excellence equals art or, in rare cases, rage. The former allows him to dream. The latter keeps him awake at night. When you see a ballplayer walking the long hall of forgotten dreams, remind him to relax. Tight players don't make it. He just needs a base hit. The next guy hits a ball that climbs the fair blue air above the right field grass. Smooth, whose glove snaps like a Venus fly trap, chugs near the foul line's fallen light, and with glove open at waist height, waits to make the basket catch. That's three outs and the little world of the diamond shifts.

Dano hurls his body on the open bench spot next to Jim and, right hand-picking, plays air guitar. Dano's a note for note guy more than a strummer. "Ya know Winkelman's Farm?" Jim asks. "It's a cool baseball story that starts with nine notes. Da da da da da dadeda da." Dano's left fingers dance across illusory strings, but he's listening to his own melody. Spikes scraping the dugout floor, a ball kicks off the screen. Dano's bowed fingers prance alertly along the fretboard. Jim says, "It's an Alex Call song; you know, from Mill Valley. He wrote," and Jim sings, "867-530 ni-e-yine." Then, Dano sings, "867-530 ni-e-yine," and Dano disappears down the bench to convene with Slick.

Slick and Dano want the Oak's lefty, Jim Brown, to pitch the seventh inning. They send Coach Jeff—vintage Oaks cap on, bobbing in his motor chair—to the mound. He takes the ball from Big Al and pats him on the butt. Jim strides in from center field to his mound of real estate. He takes the ball from Coach Jeff and warms up. His arm was warm, but not "pitching" warm. "I want to own this hill," his body says by the way his feet rake and fill in the hole before the pitching slab; "and I feel good."

Jeff whirls in his motorized chair and takes a Sunday drive back to the dugout. He spins the cart around and resumes watch at the bench's end. Players' diamond eyes peel layers as lids lift and peer above water into the game while sweating it out. Dano saunters by, "Good job, Coach Jeff."

Baseball players try not to let heat melt them down. Players think baseball sun makes them young again. Yet, unknown elements can deceive even the greatest intention. Mr. James Brown sways, twists, and fires three nasty strikes. Jim Brown, as most of the Oaks call him, tosses a first pitch that tumbles like a lead weight—a sinker—to the next batter. A feeble grounder to the rookie. Brown covers first base with his outstretched glove arm. "Here!" Exuberance ear to ear. Brown's gold glove's as roomy as a Cadillac convertible, and the rookie flips the ball to his teammate. "Out," cries Blue.

James Brown says, "That's what I'm talking about," on his way back to the hill. He's a round man. Dense-boned. The round-faced left-hander, with a wide forehead, strides in slow motion. Back on the mound now, he throws another curve in the dirt. The hitter scratches his head and glares through narrowed and blurred eyes. The hitter leans forward,

70

and his eyes dart outside. Jim Brown delivers a pitch on the inside corner. Hitter waits for a curve, and the pitch incinerates the outside ragged edge of the swollen strike zone. For strike three, he leaves the batter wondering where the ball came from, never knowing if it's a strike till it's already passed by.

"That's three," sighs Blue.

It's as if the temperature drops ten degrees. True relief from Jim Brown gives the Oaks a fighting chance.

To no avail. The Oaks can't muster enough runs and the Napa team wins by four.

After the game, the teams begin the rituals of shaking hands, patting backs, rounding up bats, and packing spikes. The players drag their aching frames away for home and for the awaiting formations of ice: cubes, trays, wraps, tall and frosty drinks, bowls, packs, and even handfuls of frozen peas on the back of their necks, shoulders, elbows, and knees—for the pure decontamination of game grime.

Dano spots Jim sitting alone on the bench. He's staring straight ahead as if communing with the ghosts of his past with eyes like two smoldering campfires. Dano says aloud—to Jim and anybody within a hundred feet, "Jim! Today was your baptism of fire." He slows the phrase down to allow it to sink into Jim's brain, "today   was   your   baptism of fire— you played your first *complete* game and found your composure in a 105-degree inferno! Today you escaped doubt's unruly kiln."

Jim's eyes now shine like two opals as he looks upward at his coach, long face dripping sweat, no longer grinding his teeth. "Thanks, Dano," he says. "Now you're a *baseball player*," Dano adds with a loud oomph, "in *any* weather, on *any* field."

71

Ojos—*para Tom Ribbecke*

Los ojos ven todos los colores del día largo de béisbol: los azules profundos y lejos, carpetas del campo y líneas laterales, líneas de tiza y tierra roja cuidada—soleada, regada y rastrillada hasta suave, luego maltratada con menos respeto.

Y los miles de campos, donde un jugador grande se disuelve y nada se queda menos sus ojos, el guante, y la pelota de béisbol—a veces con sus propios ojos, mientras se raya en su trozo del cielo.

Él se mueve a través de la pelota—en la carrera por dondequiera que vaya, así va el jardinero. La pelota es el conejo o el zorro; el jardinero es el sabueso.
Cuando sus ojos la siguen en su guante, su cuerpo se materializa en luz.

Eyes —for Tom Ribbecke

Eyes see all colors of the long baseball day: the deep far blues, carpets of infield and sidelines, chalk lines and tended red dirt—sunbaked, watered and raked smooth, then roughed up with less regard.

And the miles of outfields, where a large player dissolves and nothing remains but his eyes, the glove, and the baseball—sometimes with its own eyes, as it streaks into his field of sky.

He moves through the ball—on the run wherever it goes, so goes the outfielder. The ball is the rabbit or fox; the outfielder, the hound. When his eyes follow it into his glove, his body materializes into light.

Blues de Cuádriceps Adoloridos

Tengo los blues de cuádriceps adoloridos.
Los blues verdaderos de cuádriceps adoloridos.
No puedo ir al juego hoy;
apenas puedo bajar las escaleras.

Y ayer la democracia por poco se muere.
Allá en Washington.
Entonces, tengo una casa caótica.
Y las cosas no andan bien ahora.
Tengo los blues de cuádriceps adoloridos.

Tal vez falté ver la puesta de sol
y arrojar la pelota bajo cielo.
No puedo empujar demasiado estos días
porque la vida está empujando lo suficiente de todos modos.

Sigo aguantando.
Aguantando
hasta que mi día en el sol llegue
sin los blues de cuádriceps adoloridos.

No quiero más blues de cuádriceps adoloridos.

Sore Quad Blues[x]

I got some sore quad blues.
The real sore quad blues.
I can't make the game today,
can barely walk downstairs.

And yesterday democracy almost died.
All the way back in Washington.
So, I got a chaotic house.
And things ain't easy now.
I got the sore quad blues.

Maybe I got to miss the setting sun
and throwing the ball under the sky.
Can't push too hard these days
cause life's pushing hard enough anyway.

I just keep holding on.
Holding on
till my day in the sun comes around
without the sore quad blues.

I don't want any more sore quad blues.

Still, one game does not a make a player. More challenges lie ahead for Jim. Practice ensures him a few catacombs of sleep without frequent inner earthquakes jarring him awake, as he rewinds frames of *poorly* played games. Tossing all night, he sourly spits out bad calls, errors, and hits that didn't fall, as if ancient wolves indeed howled in the room. Somehow between those fitful nights and the next time he shows up, the midnight phantoms become extinct and become, instead, instinct. The next time on the diamond, he may pick the grounder up—that once froze him. He gets the out call on the throw home and pulls the inside pitch— to right field for a base hit instead of popping out.

Like REBL 80-year-old veteran Lowell Stalbaum said, "Jim, you're playing like a young man again. But you need to see the ball to hit it. Don't *think* about hitting it."

*****

The time has come to face the team the Oaks must play at their best. The faint fragrance of Old Spice catches a few players' attention as the team lumbers behind the mesh into the dugout at G. Park. Jim notices it right away as he passes through the hollow gate. Otto must have been here but he can't be found. A plastic grocery bag sits on the bench and standing upright beside it, a two-toned bat. Closer inspection reveals an unfinished ash handle and an unblemished jet-black barrel. Jim picks it up and marvels. "It's a 33" Akadema." Around the sweet spot, a sleeve of paper bag is wrapped. "For Jim, the thin handle will give you more bat speed. You're still swinging underwater. Stop day dreaming and living in the past. Try this out. You'll feel the difference." "It's from Otto," Jim exclaims and a few players, suiting up and digging into their packs for gloves and spikes, barely glance at the scene.

In the bag was Otto's unnumbered jersey and a postcard with a photo of Candlestick Park in its baseball symmetry. Jim reads it aloud. "Time for me to retire from the game. I have a major flair of plantar fasciitis and for reasons outside of baseball, this year hasn't been any fun. Sorry fellas, I don't like goodbyes. Good luck, Oaks. – Otto."

Nobody said much, most of the team knew Otto was off kilter this year. It happens to most players at one time or another: illnesses, injuries, divorces, deaths, births, jobs in upheaval, restorations and relocations. Sometimes simultaneously more than one. These local ballparks provide a chance to live within an alternate reality. Some things you can't escape no matter where you are. You are still here. Or there as the case may be.

The Oaks went back to the business of getting ready to play the Dragons who were already on the field, lined up in two rows— throwing. Jim felt relieved and, at the same time, a tad miffed. He relaxed his shoulders and stuffed the new bat into his gear bag and pulled from it his thick handled 34" signature Jackie Robinson. He holds it upright and spies the splotchy Louisville label and reverses it to note the faded JR4 on the end knob. He had kept this bat around since the days of Joe and the sandlots. For luck, he'll swing it today against the Dragons.

Though he had learned one necessary ingredient of a baseball player from Otto—poise in the line of fire—he doesn't hang on his every word. Someone cried, "It's a new ball game." Slick booms and Dano echoes, "Get out on the field, gentleman. We've got to play our best game today." "These guys aren't good for nothing."

After their warmups, the Dragons gather en masse, break, and angle to their positions on the field. Jim's been through his baptism of fire but this is the Dragons, the best team in REBL baseball.

The last time these teams played, Rich Murray hit a ninth inning home run that spoiled Slick's pitching gem and cost the Oaks a victory. The Dragons, perennial champions in the REBL, are run by former vintner Allan Green. Rich Murray plays first base and bats fourth. Rich Murray, who played first base for the San Francisco Giants in the early '80s, styles in about 6'5" with a plentiful smile. Mike "Tiny" Felder, a 10-year major leaguer and another former Giant, switch hits at will, no matter which arm the pitcher throws at him. And he runs and fields as easily as the velvet hands of Lester Young fingered the keys of his saxophone.

Jesus Renteria, the Dragon's catcher, one of three Renteria brothers to play for the Dragons, fires the baseball down to second base; Ralph slides headfirst. "Safe," cries the umpire, Blue.

In a Dragons' game, humor leaps over the diamond. Jim doesn't understand every word, but thinks he hears them exclaim about a base runner, "He runs like a turkey with his head turned sideways." The Oaks' "Redwood Hannan" knocks a long fly double past the glove of the right fielder. Hisses, cackles, and bass-low rumbling and grumbling adds a bit of baroque to the score in the Dragon's dugout. The Rookie, a pinch running, hauling into third, sees the coaching box then palms up from Slick. Jim thought he could have scored. Slick played it safe. Piercing cheers of hungry hawks ascend from the line of Dragons gripping the dugout mesh. "Stay outside the chalk, in foul territory," Slick says. That way if the ball hits you, you won't get called out." Third base is, just like they say, "the hot corner" for the runner as well. Anticipation in overdrive. Baseball's angels swirl around home plate. The competitor rises out of the ashes of doubt. Jim's mouth is watering for the roast beef and chef's salad.

But they're not on the menu. Only Cream of Wheat this time. A soft pop to the shortstop for the third out, and the Dragons gather their wits at the bat rack.

Practice is one thing; games are another. Games run hotter. Oversimplify fun, and a pivotal moment escapes one's grasp for an error. Or a crash between the eyes. Baseball is focus and repetition designed to master a moment of surprise. How does one react to something repeated many times yet is never the same? More practice, more innings.

Mike Felder stands at the plate. He's swinging left-handed. The rookie, on his toes, on the outside, plays eight feet off the line. Over and over, Dano yells at him, "Play on the line; the next swing is coming right at you—get ready." I'm sure the rookie didn't hear Dano. Why couldn't the rookie hear Dano? Who could *not* hear Dano? He stays put.

On the inside, Jim has checked out. He must have been listening to a song in his head. Or maybe he was deaf to any other sound than the swing of his bat— his JR4 didn't connect today. The problem is, he's playing first base and thinking about his hitting. The sounds of his ground outs have become too common. He's making contact but they aren't dropping. He's listening to the grid that doesn't go away cause his stats are on the REBL.org website: Seven strike outs, eight errors, four walks, three runs, a stolen base, and a batting average—.120—a dud that everyone— by now—expects.

Next pitch, Mike (Tiny) Felder blasts a liner between the rookie and the line. Smooth did hear Dano and backs up in short right. Tiny rounds first and holds. In the silence, the pro and the rookie look out at the field that lies before their squinting eyes. One knows. One sees and doesn't know. The rookie plays here. But he wasn't born here like Mike Felder. Tiny doesn't *"play"* here. He was *"born"* here in the 19th Century.

Jim once met a player at the Giants Ball Dude/Dudette try-out Camp in San Francisco. She told Jim that she was a lifelong baseball fan and an on-and-off player who was born in a station wagon in a baseball stadium parking lot. Her story made Jim think that Felder was probably born on a baseball field at home plate or at least on third base itching for home instead of the parking lot. Those rings of sparkling diamonds that circle his keen eyes speak volumes in the man we call Tiny. He's already set his spyglass on home plate.

Next pitch, Tiny, steals second, sliding: "Safe." He's back up on his feet. Brushing down his uniform like he was a thoroughbred that bolted from the barn, he had raced to a different part of the world.

Players paint the dirt with their spikes, step forward, and rise and fall on the balls of their feet. Big Al pitches and pulls the string we call a changeup. A high pop-up to medium right, Smooth moves in, baskets the catch, and fires it to third base to try to get Felder, who—buried under the swirls of dust, prone to the ground and flat on his side—slides under the tag beating the ball. He's up again and the ritual continues. Infield dirt cascading from his head to his shoes. He swipes his cap on his thigh.

Seconds pass in drops of sweat and dust. Players reset—and the next pitch is on its way. High fly to left field that's falling on a drop and heading for a clean patch of green. Tim Hannan digs and foots it down.

81

His long limbs outstretch; you see that red cap following the ball. Feet, waist, and shoulders twist around with both hands up, leather hand open; the ball slams into the redwood grove in his glove. No throw home will get him. Tiny tags up and scores; that's how it is when Dragons slay. A single run, followed by the flourishing wheat fields and bunches of harvested runs that follow.

Oaks bounce back. Dano whacks a double to right on the first pitch. Starkey, a utility spark plug, pinch runs for Dano. Bobo, the Oaks' clean-up lefty, bulks Incredible Hulky at the plate. A buzzing yard lapses into a silent adrenalin watch. Like horses when one of the herd escapes, not one eye blinks. As he turns on the pitch, the nose under his hat has already dropped down on the ball like a horse sniffing a bucket full of oats. At the crack of impact, the cowhide etches triple on the sweet spot of the barrel of Bobo's Louisville Slugger. A high pearl deep into right field, Jim, now coaching first base, watches it arc in the sparse cirrus clouds. The fielder backpedals, and it's over his head! Starkey scores. Bobo digs around second and bellies and scrapes across the dirt to third. He grabs for the bag like a swimmer for a life raft. It's a brand-new ballgame.

In a moment of a player's choosing, the play within the play reveals the person. Later in the game, Tiny and Jim stand side by side at first base. With eyes as calm as summer ponds, clear pools not shrunken by drought, but brimming, Tiny says, "We're up by six runs." Tiny's eyes quiet with kindness. Perhaps he knows the win and smells the familiar aromas of home cooking. Leading off first base, he turns and looks the restless rookie in the eyes again: "I'm not going to run on you, man." Meaning he's not going to steal second base out of mercy for Jim and for

82

the Oaks. It's his and the Dragon's show of respect. A quiet world of breeze and ease sweeps over Jim. Not all players, not all teams play by that code of honor.

"Relax, Man," Tiny says.

The next hitter lines one deep into the leftfield gap to the fence. Tiny scores all the way from first. Dragons win.

After the games, both sides line up. The rookie catches on like a caboose. They walk the line shaking, fisting, elbowing, hugging, high fiving, whatever it takes to cool the inner competitor. Players learn the practice of tempering rivalries by this postgame ritual.

No rivalry for the rookie, though; he's elated to be on the same field as the Dragons. He rose to the occasion, surprised himself, and played the best team. But still the quiet of his bat haunts his happiness. No hits. He's thinking he'd better follow The Swede's lead on this one and spend some time at Hinkle's batting cage. At any rate, his mind clicks away in the grid of the mesh about his stats, but he's in a kind of bliss from the release of peptides and activated opiate receptors that have lent him a temporary analgesic high from Sunday baseball. He realizes that sometimes, the deniability of the cold facts that don't seem so isolated anymore—on this field, with these teammates—carries its own repair for falling short of his own potential, just as a cruise or a cold beer rejuvenates others.

Some guys don't come out of the dugout if the game was played bitterly. It shows up on occasion as an absence on the field. Most guys show respect to the other team's players. Especially the Dragons.

La Puesta de Sol Está Teñida Azul en Llamas

El campamento roe los huesos de un día fracasado,
en medio de velas y linternas.
Los jugadores se zambullen sobre cobijas desenrolladas
bajo los sonidos del silencio en sí, se reclinan, y crujen como hojas caídas.

Bolsas de hielo se amontonan sobre brazos, hombros, y muñecas;
un jadeo en la luz resplandeciente es el único comentario humano.
Negro de ojo, cayéndose sobre caras sudadas, se desvanece por
la fogata abundante.

Siluetas se juntan alrededor de la luz de fuego.
Ojos se revelan.
No ganamos por revertir el marcador.

Ganamos por nuestro orgullo,
y la alegría nunca se pierde.

Sunset is Blues'd with Fire

The campground gnaws on the bones of the failing day,
amid candles and lanterns.
Players dive onto unrolled bedding
under quiet's own sounds, lean back, and rustle like fallen leaves.

Ice bags pile high on arms, shoulders, and wrists;
a gasp in the lambent light is the only human comment.
Eye black, running down sweaty faces, disappears near
the swarming campfire.

Silhouettes gather around the firelight.
Eyes come out of hiding.
We won't win by reversing the score.

We won by our pride,
and joy never loses.

**REBL Hall of Famer Michael Fassio, a teammate on
Don DeCordova's Redwood Empire World Series team in 1993.**

Vientos de Béisbol de Primavera

El viento le sopla la pelota de falta hacia atrás,
cayéndose dentro de la línea de base, justo
como aquel pop-up de Napa en el viento una tarde.
Es la tercer presencia del corredor. En el campo, es el viento,
la tierra, y el fuego de los jugadores que hacen el juego.

Béisbol en el viento de la primavera.
es una brisa helada alaskeña
la mañana del primer partido.
Jugadores aparecen, balanceando bates más pesados
con tempranos, densos, oscuros y nuevos anillos de crecimiento.

El otoño lleva al caballo pesado del viento veraniego sobre su espalda,
pero la primavera sirve los hielos invernales. Vientos silbantes tocan
melodías con flautas estancadas a los huesos rígidos y helados de los
jugadores.

Tornados de polvo remolinean y molestan a los residentes del plato el
domingo por la mañana. Tornados ciegan al receptor, Blue; aun los
bateadores forrajean sus párpados por piedritas de arena.

El movimiento del bate apresura el aire turbulante,
revolviendo el uno rare momento de tranquilidad..

Cuando la sangre calienta al bateador por haber corrido las bases,
el viento engaña y confunde igualmente.

Sigue el viento del océano, el olor del aliento de una gaviota, mientras los
vendavales soplan con fuerza a través del campo. El jardinero izquierdo
valsa bajo alas transparentes. Lo ve; entonces, sus pies dan un paso al
costado.

Chocó contra la cerca esa mañana. Contuvimos nuestro aliento un día de
finales la primavera en Un Lugar Para Jugar.
La pelota voló por la línea de falta; se abandona al impactar.

Baseball Winds of Spring

The foul ball blows back,
landing inside the baseline, fair
like that Napa pop up in the wind one afternoon.
It's the third presence. On the field, it's the wind, earth,
and fire of players that make the game. Water keeps them alive.

Baseball in the spring wind.
is an Alaskan freeze-breeze
the morning of the first game.
Players showing up swinging heavier bats
with early, and dense, dark, and new growth rings.

Autumn carries the heavy horse of summer wind on its back,
but Spring serves winter's ice cubes. Whistling winds
play tunes with flutes stuck to players' stiff and frozen bones.

Dust tornadoes swirl and disturb the Sunday morning residents of home
plate. Twisters blind the catcher, Blue; even the hitters forage their eyelids
for sand pebbles.

The bat's swing rushes turbulent air,
stirring the one rare moment of stillness.

When the blood warms the batter from running the bases,
the wind fools and confounds just the same.

Follow the ocean wind, the smells of gull's breath, as gales bluster across
the outfield. The left fielder waltzes under transparent wings. He sees it;
then, his feet take sideways steps.

He crashed into the fence that morning.
We held our breath one late spring day at A Place to Play.
The ball sailed past the foul line; it was abandoned upon impact.

No necesitaban a un compañero de equipo ni una barandilla para ayudar
la cerca de campo. El jardinero izquierdo se presentó una vez más.

En menos de los pocos segundos que tardó la mezcla de mirlos en
dispararse desde el jardín central a los huecos de la tribuna, fue

el siguiente lanzamiento.

Persigue a las alas chirriantes de los mirlos
desde los huecos justo por el muro del campo derecho central .
El viento soplándose dirigió el balon sobre la cerca.
DeCordova lo llamó "la corriente en chorro."
"Golpeó la pelota en la corriente en chorro y el balón salió fuera," dijo.

Junto a familia y amigos,
pasando el tiempo por detrás del plato,
el viento de béisbol cubre y abraza

el amargo bu occasional
en el medio de los sonidos del gran aplauso.

¿Brisa? ¿Brisa? ¿Escuchas, brisa más bella?
Despiértate y escapa en los caballos appaloosa corriendo a toda velocidad.

They were not in need of a teammate nor a handrail to brace their stride across the grass, back under the shivering trees lining the outfield fence.

The left fielder stood once again. In less than the few seconds it took for the jumble of darting blackbirds to spiral from center field into the hollows of the grandstands, it was

next pitch.

Chase the blackbirds' squeaking wings
from the hollows of the grandstands over right center field wall.
The wind blowing out sent the ball over the fence.
DeCordova called it, "the jet stream."
"He hit the ball in the jet stream and out it went," he said.

Along with family and friends
shooting the breeze behind home plate,
baseball wind drapes and embraces

the occasional sour boo
amidst the cracklings of collective cheers.

Breeze? Breeze? Are you listening, fairest breeze?
Wake up and escape on wild appaloosas thundering past.

Both Sides of the Diamond

An unusually hot morning for usually cool and windy Petaluma. Oaks and Mariners. No greetings emit from little Eddie on the sun-warmed spot of the short wall. He's probably back at G. Park, wondering where the Oaks are. I'm sure somebody told him the last game was in Petaluma. We're hopeful he'll find another game to pass the time away. Coach Jeff has taken the day off, too, but Ashley the Muse hops around greeting the team; shriek, squeak, bellow, grin—she knows which dugout she's in.

Jim's running on tired legs from the rookie's journey, but they're sluggish legs of a game-worn horse, not the languid legs of the lame horse that showed up back in April. The entire team has crossed over the bridge into the season's final game. Next, he hears who's pitching, catching, etc., and he's starting first base. Later, he'll get on base and enjoy that marvelous view of time in slow motion; the next hitter moves him along and he's running the bases past his winded conclusion to home plate.

A mile from historic downtown, Petaluma High School, cozied among colorful rows of rural-tinged backyards, welcomes the loyal Oaks dragging in for the season's finale. Local residents smile and wave, jogging past the tennis courts and gymnasium on the way to the sparkling pool that's turned as blue as a cobalt gemstone in the deep end. The thinly designed dugouts were built like theater aisles; a big guy can't squeeze by without feet turning sideways.

Late in the game, Cookie comes in to pitch. He's walking slowly like he's leading his horse to a watering hole. He's the horse and rider both. The centerfielder, Bobo, signals the outfielders over for a word.

91

"Get ready to run," he says. A minute later, the marathon begins, and the outfielders run like beagles chasing blue jays throughout the outfield grass. And in a moment not of a player's choosing, the play creates the player. Cookie throws the fly ball pitch but Bobo carries a focused lens inside his seeing-eye glove. He runs a sinking liner down and dives onto the thick lawn. A crop of green smears across his uniform. Both sides of the diamond cheer.

The sun rose early—as sweet as the golden drop of autumn that crispens the air—on the morning of that last game against the superb Mariners. But the Oaks' defense melted down in the first inning, and the Mariners piled up runs. However, in the ninth, with two outs, the megaphone voice behind Slick's razor-sharp eyes notes a wildness in the pitcher. "Make him throw a strike," he booms to an Oaks player swinging at bad pitches.

Jim pulls the Otto bat from his bag for his last ups of the season. He figures it won't hurt to try something new. He hasn't given the bat much thought since the Dragons game. It's a little out of his comfort zone, a thin handle in his large hands. It almost feels like a golf club. Swinging on the first pitch, he laces the ball foul near the first base line. "Whew, quick," he says to no one, when someone's always listening. Holding off on a few wayward pitches, and a called strike, he works the count to three and two. His eyes widen as the next pitch arrives a ball's width below his knees—dead center of the plate. In that split second of —to swing or to not to swing—he vies for reason over impulse. He, like everyone on both benches, had heard Slick. He wasn't going to make the third out by swinging at a low—pitcher's pitch. Blue senses the moment of drama and bellows, "Ball four," and points open handed to first base.

Jim will have to wait till next year to swing—The Thin Man—already the bat's nickname.

Smooth strides to the plate and slows the game down even further by walking on four pitches. Ralph Smith's up next, standing in the box with catcher's wisdom pounding in his heart. He looks up from his practice swings, eyes glaring, daring the pitcher to throw that feeble strike a pitcher sometimes throws when he's off track and needs to find the plate again.

It arrives like a love letter in the mailbox. Ralph smokes a skyward star over the left fielder's head and Jim and David visit the corners of the world and arrive home safely. The bench erupts in raised arms and flashes of light.

Tim Redwood Hannan, unblinking, strides to the plate and stands in the grove of his own convictions. Far too many to list here but one of them is to hit the ball as far as he can. The team rushes out from the dugout and lines up outside the mesh. They notice the grass growing taller and sense they'll have more to chomp on. Hannan's getting the follow-up-to-wildness pitches, polishing the corners. He's swinging hard enough to send the ball into next year. On the final pitch, he routes those long arms across the strike zone. But the ball blurs through a hole in his bat, avoiding the shock of contact with Hannan's lumber.

The game and the season are over.

Mientras Arrojábamos al Atardecer

El béisbol es un eclipse;
un fragmento de luna se desvanece.
Untamos naftalina a los guantes con pesadumbre.
Mi amigo Joe y yo jugamos a la pelota,
lanzando a través del golpeteo de respiración y cuero.
Brazos tiran y lanzan por susurros de sombras—
uno impulsado por la aflicción, el otro por la lealtad.
Doyle Park, una noche de diciembre.

Arrojamos con la majestad sin fin de verde,
paisajes abismales ondulantes
mientras el patrón del silencio zumba
la tristeza y las sombras nocturnas de luto.

Bases desgastadas, derrotadas por millones—
el polvo fantasmal de las líneas de tiza.
Gradas vacías y escaleras y estrellas—gritos ahogados
forman parte de esta tierra una vez joven.
Un desenfoque que no flaqueamos o faltamos. Strike.

Una neblina de luz rosada con un resplandor sedoso
se desliza por detrás de primera base.
La mejilla suave de la cara de creación
absorbe los colores de noche exprimidos en vino.

Linternas de luces del parque parpadean en
toques circulares por robles del siglo pasado.
Vapores de neblina reducen su brillo de aguardiente.
Latidos de corazón bordean el campo en tiempo
lejos e ininterrumpido.
Un desenfoque que no flaqueamos o faltamos. Strike dos.

Nosotros los hombres mayores,
hombres jorobados y callados,
secamos las lágrimas de nuestros ojos oscuros y ahogados.
Arrojamos a través de la noche en un trance ferviente.

94

While We Threw at Dusk

The baseball is an eclipse;
a shard of moon vanishes.
Mothballed gloves smeared with gloom.
My friend Joe and I playing catch,
pitching through the patter-port sounds of breath and leather.
Arms toss and sling through sighing shadows—
one driven by grief, the other loyalty.
Doyle Park, December evening.

We throw with the endless majesty of green,
abysmal landscapes undulating
while the patron saint of silence hums
the sorrow and nightly shades of mourning.

Basepaths worn down, routed by the millions—
ghostly dust of the chalk lines.
Empty stands, and stairs, and stars—muffled cries
are of this once youthful land.
A blur we didn't flinch or miss. Strike.

A rose-light mist with silken glow
glides in from behind first base.
The soft cheek of creation's face
soaks in the colors of night squeezed into wine.

Torches of park lights blink on
circular splashes in last century's oaks.
Fog's vapors slow their brandy glow.
Heartbeats rim the field in far unbroken time.
A blur we didn't flinch or miss. Strike two.

We older men, hunched and quiet men,
swipe the tears from our dim-drowned eyes.
Throw through the night in fervid trance.

Uno impulsado por la aflicción lee las señales,
uno por la lealtad tararea "Taps" por inocencia negada, asimismo.

El guante en la mano de Joe se congela, tan quieta como una piedra.
Tiro la pelota, pero ni siquiera puede volar un cuervo
de cabeza en una muralla que no existe.
Un desenfoque que no flaquea o falta él. Strike tres.

En el plato, nos estrechamos las manos calentadas por el fuego,
comprendiendo la representación ilusoria pero obvia
aflojada en el crepúsculo.
El primero de muchos que nacimos para ver marcharse.

One driven by grief reads the signs,
one by loyalty hums "Taps" for innocence further denied.

The glove on Joe's hand freezes, as still as stone.
I hurl the baseball, but even a raven cannot fly
headlong into a wall that doesn't exist.
A blur he doesn't flinch or miss. Strike three.

At home plate, we shake hands warmed by the pitching fire,
fathoming the delusional but obvious rendering loosened in the twilight.
The first of many we were born to see go.

Extra Innings

After the Mariner game, Bobo's family joined the team at the ballpark, and fertility blossomed in the long dreads of Bobo's children. Kids of all ages carried in platters of food: barbequed chicken, bowls of fruit, potato salad, gravy, garden tomatoes, French bread. Soft drinks chilling in ice broken out of coolers, thermoses emptied of coffee. In the hazy autumn sky, players' laughter sustained itself like the strings of a symphonic finale while the sun revealed shadows of fatigue.

In the ballgame, the guys played in slow time, where real time became the hurried illusion. It's a code; a player dares not look over his shoulder to smell the barbeque, or he might miss the split second he needs the most to make a play that's passing right under his nose. Yet, that last day was different. Pepper, onions, and barbeque sauce seduced the famished team.

Outside the chain link fences, serious times lurked like paparazzi, yet righties, lefties, and libertarians alike shared food, jokes, and conversation. Jim, the rookie-no-more said, "Last week the country hit the lowest economic bottom since the Great Depression." "That's right," Hannan replied, "They should abolish the IRS and start all over." Well said from the libertarian candidate who ran for California Attorney General in 2010 and received 17,957 votes.

With the election coming up, the vocal team barked about who might become the next president. Dano hollered, "Research just released said this country is 40 percent racist and will never elect a black president." Jim protested, "I thought this country had evolved beyond that." Then Dano retorted, "Yeah, for guys like you and me who went through the '60s. But it's a lot bigger of a country than us."

David. Smith, sunglasses on, steered the team around the next bend, "Baseball is physics and timing. What happens at the point of impact is what counts."

Jim Linehan's empty-gloved hand raises a water bottle to the fusion of Oaks. Remembering, too, his friend he called The Swede, Joe Lindquist, RIP. "Does anybody have Hinkle's phone number?"

The team filtered out to their cars as a breeze stole into the ballpark, followed by gangs of crows flocking into the trees.

Craw and caw, silence catching their cries—they drop, wings arced, flying in half circles, and take back the ruddy diamond.

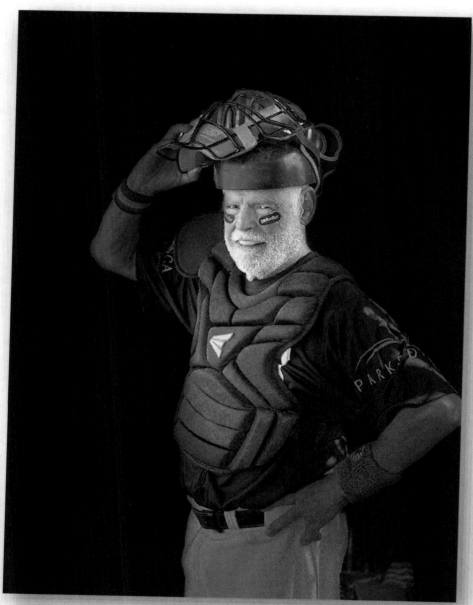

Rich Hinkle, who plays all nine positions on the field,
gets ready to catch.

Epilogue

The availability of adult baseball leagues has blossomed into fruition in the 21st century. In Sonoma County, California, the Redwood Empire Baseball League evolves from year to year, decade to decade.

The following year, REBL restructured the league and the Oaks played in a 55-plus league. They won the championship with a playoff victory over a team called Dirt Dogs. A lot of those players packed up from Golis Park and flew to Arizona to play in the Men's Senior Baseball League World Series, winning the championship ring they have sought for decades. Slick, Dano, and Cookie maintained G. Park until Cookie retired and Dano moved out of the area.

After the 55+ came the 65+. Called the Legends League. In 2014, a new team evolved. A few guys formed a team of castoff players from folded teams and renamed it the Blues. Now the league has both the Jazz, and the Blues. Ballplayers from the Oaks, included stalwart David Smith, Wayne Pellow, Lowell Stalbaum, and Willard Ferrell. Others, like Rick Hinkle, Jim Sullens, your's truly, and Rick Harmon, joined from the Dirt Dogs, and other players, like Jim Brown, Ladd Miyasaki, Greg Peterson, and Rick Mercurio, formed its core. Later, they would add guys like Tom Ribbecke, a world class instrument maker who creates beauty in the world, and Jim Maresca, an actor who played Lord Macduff and cut Macbeth's head off in the final act of a Sonoma County Shakespeare production.

Cincinnati draftee, Rick Hinkle—a multi-faceted guy, including the realms of writing and music—was to become the Blues' professional in residence.

103

Often 10 runs down but still laughing, the Blues had become a rolling band of creative souls with zero wins and 21 losses. A 55+ team dedicated to playing and keeping veterans in the game.[xi] They didn't win any games, but they always showed up on photo day, smiling from ear to ear because they played baseball for another year.

A few years later, Don DeCordova returned to Sonoma County and created a team called the Vets. Don retired from actively managing in the REBL in 2021, but he still builds tournament teams to play in Palm Springs, San Diego, Las Vegas and, of course, the gemstones of excellence, the spring training fields in Arizona.

Don will always say, with eyes as steady as a fair and impartial judge, "My life is baseball," and you will watch the unfolding of a gold-leafed map from a deep dugout of acceptance and translatable joy.

Donny D invited Jim to play in the magic 1993 World Series. That was the year they played games ASU and at in Scottsdale Stadium, the second home of the San Francisco Giants. Something extra happens when you play in those ballparks. Especially in a warm Arizona night game. Your curveball breaks a few inches more. The mound feels like butter. The ball practically stops in the air when you're up at bat.

DeCordova and his wife Shari are lifers in the REBL. You'll know him by his many fans and the cowbells that chortle with dignity at the games.

Dick Giberti, who turned 86 in the summer of 2023 is the patriarch of the league and is still getting batters out. His example lends credence to the phrase, "live longer, play baseball." In his outing on July, 2023, he pitched five innings, allowed three hits, no runs, and struck out seven. Coach Jeff has retired, like his father Jon McGraw, but we still see him driving his cart on the field as he shakes hands with the players. David Smith and Al Surges are still active players. The rookie, Jim, in his final year hit .292 with zero errors. He retired after that 2021 season but is getting the itch that never goes away—to play baseball in a league with real parks, real umpires with awe-inspiring teammates and exceptional players. Tim Redwood Hannan has retired from baseball and is still practicing law. Hall of Famer Larry Hendrickson played organized baseball every year since 1968, and at 72, he still pitches for 55-plus and 65-plus leagues with Allen Green's Dragons. Handfuls of players retire from senior baseball and come back to the fields once again after a long summer of watching games on TV.

The senior 65-plus Legends division rivalry of teams always leads back to the Dragons. Yet the Jazz went undefeated one year and wrestled the trophy away. Then another challenger, the Emeralds, an all-star team that plays in San Rafael's, Albert's Park, came along to raise the stakes even higher: The Emeralds won the championship in their first year. Then the Dragons came back and clawed the trophy away in 2023.

Jim "Lefty" Brown, and number one fan, Little Eddie, have passed away, as have former friends and teammates Ralph Smith, Phillip Salazar, and Steve McMahon. Greg Peterson, who always brought his mother to games and whose disappearance remains a mystery, is the most recent and disturbing to join the Baseball Infinity Club. They found his car burning along a highway without a trace of him inside, and he has not been found.

Lou Patler, a poet and award-winning author—named "One of America's newest diplomats" by Marin County Independent Journal—has been an active player in various Senior Baseball Leagues and was part of a team of 14 American baseball players that traveled to Cuba. On that journey, they played a Cuban women's national champion team, ranked first in Cuba and second in the world. They lost the first game and won the second. He most recently played in the 2022 Senior World Series with teammate Ralph Leef, who is now 75 and playing in a 58+ league in Denver, Colorado.

Jim has played from 92-94, and 2006-2021, missing a couple of years for health issues unrelated to baseball (though the website shows only 10 years) with the Cubs, Red Sox, Dragons South, Oaks, Dirt Dogs, and the Blues. Like every other player in the league, he carries a highlight reel in his head, has played with the best, and has made a lot of friends.

The teams regroup over the winter. Some players drop out; more sign up. Liability waivers go out to players and doctors are consulted. Others come back after a year off. Games begin in April. The REBL beat goes on.

News Flash. Allan Green sent invitations to form a new league. A 73+ with three teams. 10-12 games. Wednesdays at 10:00. I'm in. David Smith is in.

Decirle Adiós

Radios para autos a todo volumen para las cabinas de peaje.
Por detrás de las monedas y agradecimientos,
él cargó el ambiente de hola y adiós.

Lon Simmons creció del paisaje de San Francisco,
como un clarinete bajo en un cuarto lleno,
y surgió a las aceras, cafés, y tabernas.

En las estratas saltarines y cambiantes de la rutina
ascendente-descendente, al zumbido de llantas del vecindario, Lon
se sentó al otro lado del pasillo en los comienzos y paradas por monedas
de los autobuses electrificados acercándose a la acera
con las puertas dobles retrocedidas,
invitando a extraños de lugares lejanos.

En las caminatas a través de las avenidas,
fuera de los toldos de restaurantes,
cruzando mal la calle entre los autobuses estacionados, desde las puertas
de autos hasta los portones. Por las calles con la colección de La Ciudad
de corazones pasados, la voz de Lon siempre nos llevaba a casa.

Sus gritos llenaron los jardines en las tardes de sábado,
como los olores hinchados de humo de un asado dando la vuelta,
goteando sobre los carbones que quemaba mi padre.

Sus llamadas derivaban desde la esquina y se concentraban
como los cuerpos de niebla del océano estirados
encima de la mujer sonriente en La Playa del Océano.

Saltó por el hombre del acordeón con un ojo sellado,
y un salvaje ojo azul de miosotis fijado y vacío,
arrugas horizontales por su amplia frente.
Él paraba a través de décadas, con cara lejana hacia arriba
y dedos hinchados, bombeando el aliento tomado del instrumento
mientras un monito gris, disfrazado en traje rojo y gorro,
monedas coleccionadas en su taza de metal.

Tell it Goodbye

Car radios blaring for the toll booths.
Behind the swapped quarters and thank yous,
he charged the atmosphere of hello and goodbye.

Lon Simmons grew out of San Francisco's landscape,
like a bass clarinet in a crowded room,
and emerged onto its sidewalks, cafés, and taverns.

In the bouncing, shifting layers of ascending-descending grind, to the
neighborhood whirr of tires, Lon sat across the aisle on the nickel starts
and stops of the electrified busses pulling to the curb
with double doors drawn back,
welcoming strangers from faraway places.

On the walks across the avenues,
out from under the awnings of restaurants,
jay walking between the parked busses, from the car doors to the gates.
Along the streets with The City's collection of bygone hearts,
Lon's voice always brought us home.

His cries filled the backyards on Saturday afternoons,
like the smoke-swelling smells of a turning roast,
dripping over the coals that my father stoked.

His calls drifted from around the corner and massed
like the ocean's bodies of fog stretching
above the laughing lady at Ocean Beach.

It leapt past the accordion man with one eye sealed shut,
and a wild forget-me-not blue eye pinned and blank,
horizontal crinkling across his wide brow.
He stood through decades, with upward faraway face
and puffy fingers pumping the instruments' heaves of breath,
as a little grey monkey, costumed in red suit and cap,
collected coins in his metal cup.

Lon llamó a través de todo, sorprendiendo a cualquier persona que podía escuchar.

Mi familia se inclinaba hacia cualquier estación de radio AM; nuestras espinas se despertaban cuando llamaba él el homerun, "Willie Mays... y tú puedes decirle adiós."

En aquellas urgentes y perdidas charlas—con hijos adolescentes, padres, amigos de la Segunda Guerra Mundial, madres trabajadoras, hijas deportistas, y los nietos genios con las pantallas, aún no nacidos—Lon caminó a largo de los senderos agrestes a las puertas lejanas y las escaleras de Candlestick Park, su voz aflautada nos alzaba con su humor de forrajeo en el hedor que impregnaba el aire en la marea baja.

Escucha este cuento del hombre con un corazón de león, Lon Simmons; nos dirigió por los portones a un bolsillo extraordinario de la tierra—

el campo de béisbol.

Lon's calls make movement helpless while listening contained a fuller universe of endless vistas.

Lon called through it all, spellbinding anyone within earshot. My family leaning into any available A.M. Radio; our spines tingling and straightened when he called the homerun, "Willie Mays. . . and you can tell it goodbye."

On those urgent, lost natters—with teenaged sons, dads, World War II friends, working mothers, athletic daughters, and the screen-genius grandchildren that followed, not yet born—Lon walked along the rugged paths to the faraway gates and stairs of Candlestick Park, his reedy baritone lifting us with foraging humor in the permeating stench of low tide.

Hear this tale of the man with a lion's heart, Lon Simmons;
he led us through gates to an extraordinary pocket of earth—

the baseball field.

About the Author and Publisher

In the spring of his 21st year, Timothy Williams' love for poetry returned to him during a long walk on Bottle Rock Road in Lake County, California. From his wanderings that dawn, without a pen, he wrote his first poem. From there he has written: *Baseball In and Out of Time*, (Player's Edition); *Gates of Wilbur*, about Wilbur Hot Springs; *Figure on the Road*, a memoir of wildfires, historic resorts and a lost romantic era; *The Treasure of Lost Time*, a family book drawn from the hometown of his wife, Sarah Baker; and *Sleepless Fires*, a book of poems published by Running Wolf Press. In addition, his earlier collections published are: *Same Day Different Village, Spokes of a Broken Wheel*, and *Caffeine Makes you Greedy*.

Timothy created and formed Poetry Band with artist-guitarist, Kevin Haapala. They recorded one album in 2003, *Lunch at Lola's*.

Timothy's love of poetry and music, fueled his ambition to start Jaxon's Press in 2002 to augment his 30-year accounting business. What began as thank-you cards to clients and friends, grew into musical CDs by Dolly and the Lama Mountain Boys, a string quartet, called String Theories, written by his wife, composer and musician, Sarah Baker, plus his own Lunch at Lola's, a spoken-word C.D. Printed broadsides of by food writer Michele Anna Jordan, musicians Allegra Broughton and Sam Page of Solid Air, Doug Jayne and Allen Sudduth, poet Kristine Sudduth, and three poetry books by Jonah Raskin: *Letters to a Lover, Auras,* and *Storm City*. Jaxon's Press also published *Passenger Pigeons* by writer and award-winning filmmaker, Ken Rodgers.

On July 1, 2020, it published *Given Enough Time,* the book of song poems by folk legend Hugh Shacklett.

[i] Adjoined it was to the renowned Mystic Theater, originally a vaudeville theater, even a pornographic theater, called a string of names.

[ii] The semi-pro leagues, including a team from Novato, the Knickerbockers, and Santa Rosa's Rose Buds, had players like Brad Silva and Larry Hendrickson, also an Atlanta Braves minor leaguer.

[iii] This includes Jay Kibbe and others mentioned in this book.

[iv] Santa Rosa Press Democrat. Jakusho Kwong-Roshi

[v] "The Crack (or Thunk) of the Bat." Newsweek, 8-27-01, https://members.tripod.com/bb_catchers/catchers/crack_bat.htm. Accessed 7-18-23.

[vi] Williams, Niall. This is Happiness. New York, Bloomsbury Publishing, 2019.

[vii] Iritis is an inflammation of the iris in normally one eye but sometimes both.

[viii] As a multiple-year REBL Cy Young Award winner, Larry won the award in 2022.

[ix] McGraw, besides sporting a famous baseball name, plays the outfield and first base. He swings and hits loud line drives for doubles—called gappers—because they split the gap between the outfielders. His name (with added h between the o and n) resides in Cooperstown, affixing Jon to the baseball legend, John McGraw.

[x] Quadriceps. The large muscles at the front of the thigh.

[xi] David Smith, Richard Hinkle, Rick Harmon, Rick Mercurio and Wayne Pellow, shared the coaching duties. Ladd Miyasaki, Blues organic farmer is in residence, Phil Salazar, who hit one over the fence at what was once called Mountain Shadows, and Jim Sullens, who sometimes worked all night as a card dealer and showed up to play without sleep. Brad Faria and David Meyer were great players and moved on to better teams, Williard Ferrell brought his son to a practice and teammates marveled at how he threw strike after strike to the catcher. From second base! Greg Peterson who hit .364 that year, and Jim Linehan, rediscovered the art of playing first base. Lowell Stalbaum, is the second oldest player in the league next to Slick. Hinkle, and Willard logged the innings from the mound and James Brown shared spots in relief.

[xi] Curtis, Dave. "Mill Valley ballplayer leaves a bit of Marin behind during goodwill tour to Cuba." Marin Independent Journal, May 9, 2010. UPDATED July 19, 2018, www.marinij.com/news/sports/index.html. Accessed July 3, 2023.

Made in the USA
Middletown, DE
30 December 2023

46367324R00073